ALSO BY ANNA JEFFREY

The Sons of Texas
The Tycoon, Book 1
The Cattleman, Book 2
The Horseman, Book 3 (Coming Soon)

The Strayhorns
Lone Star Woman
Man of the West (w/a Sadie Callahan)

The West Texas Books
Sweet Water
Salvation, Texas
Sweet Return

The Callister Books
The Love of a Lawman
The Love of a Stranger
The Love of a Cowboy

Praise for the Novels of Anna Jeffrey

The Cattleman

"…the absolutely yummy description of Pic (Can you say Hello Cowboy?!) and a great relationship between him and Amanda made for a fabulous story that kept my interest piqued!"—*A Cup of Tea and a Big Book*

The Tycoon

"I'm looking forward to more books with this family. There's a lot going on…. not once was I bored and wished things would move faster."—*Sandy M, The Good, the Bad and the Unread*

Sweet Return

"…a master at writing a Texas tale that is not only enjoyable, but authentic as well."—*Romance Junkies*

"…another outstanding entry to Anna Jeffrey's library."—*Contemporary Romance*

"…great characters who worm their way into your heart and a spicy love story."—*All About Romance*

Salvation, Texas

"Anna Jeffrey continues to demonstrate her spectacular storytelling talents. …A first-class romantic suspense tale." —*Affaire de Couer*

"[E]xciting…Readers will enjoy Anna Jeffrey's fine thriller."
—*Midwest Book Reviews*

Sweet Water

"Jeffrey mixes just the right amounts of soft, sweet, and funny, making Agua Dulce hard to resist." —*Detroit Free Press*

"... wonderfully complex characters whose personalities are gradually revealed. There are no easy answers for any of them, but the ones they find are mostly happy and satisfyingly realistic. A pleasurable read!" —*Romantic Times*

"Sexy, tender...romantic doesn't begin to describe how wonderful this story is." —*Romance Junkies*

The Love of a Lawman

"Real characters come to life in this heart-wrenching tale littered with imperfect characters readers come to love and root for." —*Rendezvous*

"If you like well-written character-driven romances...with engaging characters and lots of internal conflict, I highly recommend *The Love of a Lawman*." —*Romance Reviews Today*

The Love of a Stranger

"Delicious...a riveting read." —*Publishers Weekly*

"Fun...a delightful solid novel." —*Midwest Book Reviews*

The Love of a Cowboy

"This book is on fire! Intense, romantic, and fiercely tender....An authentic and powerful love story."
—*Joan Johnston, New York Times* Bestselling Author

DESIRED

Miranda's Chronicles

BOOK I

ANNA JEFFREY

Please Note

This is a work of fiction. Names, characters, places, and incidents either are the product of the author's imagination or are used fictitiously, and any resemblance to actual persons, living or dead, business establishments, events or locales is entirely coincidental.

Cover design by
THE KILLION GROUP
www.thekilliongroupinc.com

ACKNOWLEDGEMENTS

As I always do, I thank my loyal friend and critique partner, Laura Renken, who writes historical romances as Melody Thomas. Thank you for your support and patience.

Chapter 1

I COULDN'T REMEMBER when I had been in a more upbeat mood. Midmorning on a sunny October day, a cloudless, brilliant blue sky and me in a fairy tale world. Heady territory where I often found myself these days. But not because good fortune had been bestowed by a fairy godmother. It was more the result of damn hard work.

On this particular day, I was standing in front of a wall of floor-to-ceiling windows in a palatial model home on the twentieth floor of Skyline, a new condominium development near downtown Fort Worth. My spirits were so high, the windows so clear, the outside view so unobstructed, I had an eerie feeling I could just step out into space and walk around out there.

Last evening's cocktail party in this very unit hung in my mind. Multimillionaire—some said billionaire— Drake Lockhart, Skyline's developer, owner and CEO of Lockhart Concepts, had hired my small company, Gala, to conduct an event to kick off Skyline's grand opening. Given the opportunity to make Gala shine right along with Skyline, I had gone all out—a truckload of lush fresh flowers, expensive champagne, top-shelf liquors and gourmet finger foods. Every drop of alcohol had been drunk and every morsel of food had been eaten. I counted the consumables a hit.

A distant sound echoing through the mostly soundproof building caught my attention and I stilled to listen. The last of my cleanup crew had just left and

I was alone. Being the only person on the top floor of an empty twenty-story building hardly gave me the warm fuzzies. The quiet was pervasive. Every unidentifiable sound made me jump. A thousand nooks and crannies existed where a bad guy might lurk. Paranoid? I couldn't deny it. I had read and heard of assaults on female Realtors in vacant houses. I wasn't a Realtor, but in this setting, I was the same as.

Behind me, my oversized tote bag sat on a gray leather L-shaped sofa that had easily seated ten people at last night's party.

I walked over to the sofa, dug my smartphone out of the bag and pressed in the cell number of Gabe Mathison, the Lockhart Concepts real estate broker I would be helping hold an open house here today.

He came on the line on the first burr. "Hey, girl."

"Hi. Where are you?"

"Just turning onto Post Oak Street in front of Skyline. You?"

"I'm in the big unit on the twentieth floor. Come on up. The front door's locked, so press the buzzer."

"On my way."

I disconnected and dropped my phone back into my bag. With a few minutes to wait, I strolled through the condo one more time, giving it one last inspection, my high heels clicking against a floor of exotic hardwood. Left over from candles I had burned earlier, the clean scents of lemon and sage floated in the air.

As I walked, I couldn't keep from admiring my surroundings. The sumptuous furnishings and accessories had been provided by one of the most exclusive furniture stores in the Metroplex and its top decorator. The place had an old-world ambiance so splendid it camouflaged the real world. But then, I reminded myself, the people who could afford to live in Skyline didn't live in the real world as I knew it.

I glanced left and right, up and down, saw no evidence that two hundred people—other Realtors and various local dignitaries and celebrities—had been here eating and drinking, dropping and spilling stuff just a few hours ago. My cleanup crew had done an excellent job. I was satisfied.

This was important to me. I had a reputation to uphold. My company presided over small events around the Dallas-Fort Worth Metroplex. Gala was only three years old, but it was becoming known as one of the best event planning companies in the area. Praise, or referrals even, from a man of Drake Lockhart's stature and reputation could help me reach an elite clientele to which I hadn't had much access before.

The front door buzzer sounded. I walked over and opened it to Gabe Mathison.

He greeted me with arms stretched wide. *"Maaa-Raaanda!"*

He sounded like Michael Buffer, that boxing and professional wrestling announcer. I couldn't keep from laughing.

Gabe and I had worked together at other Lockhart Concepts events. An avid believer in the power of positive thinking, his conversation was always peppered with quotes from self-help gurus. He was cheerful, witty and fun.

With his perfectly layered brown hair, laughing hazel eyes and stylish dress, he was cute. Well, truthfully, most of the women who met him considered him handsome. Some female acquaintance was always asking me to pass him her phone number. He reminded me of a fashion model. On his tall, slender frame, his expensive suits and power ties looked just right. He was a consummate flirt and had a long list of girlfriends.

And he makes a hell of a lot of money, an inner voice reminded me.

Mental sigh. Yeah, yeah, yeah. Another time, another life...

In my work, I met well-off—even uber-wealthy—men of all shapes, sizes and ages. Although I had seen opportunities for taking up with more than one of them, in the end, I didn't have the stomach for it. I knew a couple of women around my age who had done that. For the most part, the long-term results were not pretty. I might have been burned by romance, but I still had an old-fashioned notion of someday finding undying affection with a faithful lover.

"Long time no see," I said to Gabe, still laughing.

We touched cheeks and kissed air, then he stood back, giving me a once-over. "You're looking hot."

I put much effort and quite a bit of money into that very thing. Maintaining my appearance was part of operating expenses. Today, I had gone for the professional-and-classy look—a gray flannel pencil skirt that discreetly hugged my bottom and skimmed the tops of my knees, a tailored white long-sleeved silk blouse that showed a whisper of the lace cami I wore underneath and my new black platform peep-toe pumps for which I had paid Nordstrom's an insane price. Drake Lockhart expected a certain look from me as well as his brokers. Our appearance reflected on him and his company.

"Thank you, kind sir," I said to Gabe. "I do my best. It's a challenge for us old ladies, you know."

He winked at me and growled. "Cougar."

Gabe and I had joked about my age ever since I told him he was too young for me to date. At twenty-six, he was younger than I by two years. I had never been seriously attracted to guys younger than I was, even if only by two years. A psychologist had told me once that I was mature beyond my years because I had spent my childhood managing adult situations and I had never had a father figure in my life.

Not that plenty of men weren't around our household when I was a kid. My mom, a beauty and a charmer and a social butterfly in her youth had been a magnet for men. She had a breathy little-girl voice and an ethereal helplessness about her that made the male animal fall all over himself wanting to protect her—for about six months. Those were a few—but only a few—of the reasons she was now on her fifth husband.

But those were all things I pushed to the back of my mind most of the time. I couldn't function in the environment I tried to maintain if I let myself get lost in the jungle of my mother's problems.

As Gabe and I walked toward the window wall, he looked around the room. "Oh, man, would you look at this? Drake's pulled out all the stops this time. I've heard about this corner view. It's all he talks about."

He referred to the huge open space that was the living room, dining room and kitchen that wrapped around a corner of the building. The brilliant architectural design created a 180-degree panorama visible from almost anywhere you stood and gave the illusion of being suspended in air. This particular home, one of four, had twelve-foot ceilings and floor-to-ceiling windows the full width of the living and dining areas as well as the master bedroom and bath and one of the extra bedrooms, truly bringing the outside in.

"He sure has," I said.

He shoved one hand into his pants pocket, pushing back the tail of his dark gray suit jacket. His gaze settled on the outside view that stretched endlessly toward the western horizon and miles up and down the sinuous Trinity River. "Wow. Look at that view. Awesome. How'd you like to get up to that every morning?"

"You haven't seen it before?"

"Nope. Haven't had time to come up here."

"Why, Gabe Mathison. I'm surprised at you. You're dropping the ball."

"Been busy, babe. Movin' 'em and shakin' 'em. A lot going on right now."

Gabe was a go-getter. Ambitious and more than a little greedy. He was on his way to becoming a power player in the Metroplex real estate business. Commercial rather than residential was his game, but in the rough-and-tumble world of commercial real estate sales, sometimes there were long stretches between commissions. To support his expensive lifestyle, Gabe wasn't above spending a weekend pushing condos in one of Drake's developments. Drake would pay his brokers healthy bonuses on top of commissions for the sale of the homes in Skyline.

I would be helping Gabe this afternoon to show off a dozen Skyline model units. I would be dishing out charm and conversation and hanging on to one customer while he dealt with another.

"How much is this place?" I asked.

He scanned some papers attached to the clipboard. "Um, six thousand square feet, five bedrooms, six baths, every amenity known to man. A bargain at twelve mill."

I gaped. "*Dollars?* Are you kidding?"

One corner of Gabe's mouth quirked up and he gave me a flat look. "No, Miranda. We're talking jelly beans." He turned his eyes back to the view. "But you know Drake. I'm sure he'll negotiate on that."

"Hah," I scoffed. "What will he come down to, eleven-point-nine?"

Drake Lockhart's reputation as a tough negotiator who always stood his ground was well known.

Gabe chuckled.

I had grown up in a small rural town surrounded by farms and ranches and a population that barely scraped by. In my plebian thinking, I could not imagine paying twelve million dollars for a place to live in a high-rise building. For that much money, at the very least, land should be part of the package

"Well, I would buy it," I said, "but what would I do with my Great Dane? I don't see a place for a doghouse."

Gabe knew I didn't have a Great Dane. "Miranda, love. I'm afraid you'd have to tailor your dog to your environment."

"Hm. A tailored dog. A cat would probably find that an interesting idea."

He checked his watch. "Almost showtime. Shall we go down?"

"Let's."

We turned away from the windows and strode to the front entrance and the private elevator. Even the elevator was elegant. Dark gold-veined mirrors floated above brushed bronze wainscoting, the panels polished to a high sheen that reflected indirect lighting subtly hidden behind a cornice at the top of the walls.

We zoomed down and Gabe and I stepped out into the lobby onto a floor of gleaming snow-white marble with spidery gold veins. More marble of a pale salmon color covered the walls. A jungle of various plants and trees, some soaring to the height of several floors, beautified the whole area under a ceiling of skylights twenty floors above us.

Miranda March, the cynic, came to life. "These plants must have cost a fortune. What happens if one of them dies?"

"Good question. But I'm sure Drake's got it figured out."

This was true. Anyone acquainted with the Lockhart dynamo knew he *always* had *everything* figured out.

Paul, the concierge, met us and gestured us toward a rectangular utilitarian table and three metal chairs. Above us, a huge banner that said OPEN HOUSE spanned the width of the lobby. On the table, a plastic shopping bag and a large cardboard box awaited us. "What's this?" I asked.

Gabe picked up the shopping bag and handed it to me. "I figured we'd have an ugly table, so I stopped off and bought a tablecloth to cover it."

I pulled a slick plastic package out of the shopping bag and unfurled a burgundy brocade tablecloth with large gold tassels attached to each of the four corners. "Wow. Fancy." I laughed. "Where did you get this, at a carnival closeout?"

Gabe gave me an all-male what's-wrong-with-it look. "I got it at Goodwill."

If I had wanted a tablecloth to use at an open house showing luxurious homes, I would have gone shopping at Dillard's or Macy's. I couldn't keep from laughing more. "You are such *guy*."

He lifted the cardboard box and stepped out-of-the-way, allowing me to spread the cloth over the table. He then placed the box back on it. "This is taped shut. I don't suppose you'd have a switchblade in your purse."

"I do." I prowled inside my purse and produced a small Swiss Army knife.

He took the knife. "Women's purses. Bottomless pits."

"Shut-up. I carry it in case I have to amputate something."

Nonsensical banter with Gabe was fun.

He sliced the tape, then handed the knife back to me and lifted out a stack of portfolio-type fliers with heavy glossy covers. Inside were several pages of glossy color photographs. When it came to marketing, Drake Lockhart was the best.

"Ooh, nice fliers," I said. "Expensive. How many deals are you expecting to do today?"

"Hard to say. I'm the only one who was dumb enough to volunteer. Look outside. Great weather for golf. And there's a football game at TCU."

He was right. Balmy temperature and little wind. With good fall weather, not even shopping for a cool place to live distracted dedicated Texas golfers from weekends on the links or loyal college football fans from a Saturday afternoon game.

I reached for my bag and pulled out my Lockhart Concepts name badge that Drake had supplied me. As I pinned it on my blouse, Gabe glanced at it. "Why don't you get a real estate license, Miranda, and come to work with us? You'd knock 'em dead. I know Drake would let you hang your license."

"I've thought about it," I said, "but I like what I'm doing now."

Sometime back, Drake had offered me a desk in his brokerage if I would get a real estate license, but I had never told anyone, especially not Gabe. I couldn't see myself doing that job. The raw competitiveness of the commercial real estate business scared me. But I *had* occasionally thought about getting a real job with a regular paycheck. I had a college degree in marketing. As off-the-wall as it sounded, years ago, I had won enough scholarship money in beauty pageants to almost pay for a higher education. Those winnings plus two part-time jobs had enabled me to get a sheepskin.

After college, while I failed to connect with anyone interested in hiring me for my education, I met quite a few willing to pay me for the way I looked. So I started freelancing at what I do now and soon it became a business.

Some called Gala a froufrou enterprise that could fall apart any minute and they might be right. Though my little company was profitable, even I didn't see it as something I would do until the day I died. But unfortunately, or fortunately, depending on your point of view, nothing had pressured me to come up with a Plan B.

At present, I made enough to support myself and allow me to live reasonably well. And to the envy of some of my girlfriends who worked nine-to-five, I was my own woman. Would I be content trading that for being an employee with someone telling me what and how to do? I doubted it.

Beyond all of that, I had seen how hard Drake's people worked and the stress associated with what they did. I couldn't imagine that being as much fun as planning a party or dressing in a fashionable cocktail dress and spending a day or evening in some spotlight.

"I couldn't make the party last night," Gabe said, drawing me out of my musing. "How was it?"

"Great. You've been to my parties. Everyone likes them."

"What's not to like? River of good booze, pounds of boiled shrimp and most of Fort Worth's upper crust."

As part of my party package, I always included top-shelf liquors and my favorite caterer served nothing but fresh, premium gourmet fare. For what I charged my customers and clients, I believed they expected as much, though I economized where I could.

I gave a playful gasp. "You jest. Seriously, we had a good turnout. Everyone loved the condo and the building, too. We had endless champagne. And my fave, a chocolate fountain."

"Why do you always have a chocolate fountain at the parties you throw? You don't eat sweets."

And I didn't most of the time. I had to keep my body in shape. Besides running my small business, I was also a model of sorts. I had an agent who got me occasional gigs modeling clothing for upscale department stores in Dallas and Houston, which was fun as well as lucrative.

He also set me up as the female showpiece at this event or that. I had done car shows, boat shows, RV shows, garden shows and multiple others. I had been a hostess at a few gun shows and museum openings, even a few airplane manufacturer's events. I had a listing in the Yellow Pages. "Have cocktail dress, will travel" was my motto. I didn't intend to jeopardize any of those opportunities by gaining weight.

"The chocolate fountain isn't for me, silly," I told Gabe. "Guests love it. But I did eat one tiny strawberry dipped in chocolate. I couldn't resist."

Before Gabe and I could take our conversation further, Drake Lockhart appeared in the wide plate-glass entry and we went on alert. With him was a man who caused me to stand and stare. Drake himself was handsome enough, but his companion was utterly stunning even from a distance.

The two of them sauntered toward the back of the lobby. From Drake's hand gestures and body language, I could tell he was showing off the building. I had already seen as much of the building as I needed to, so I let my eyes feast on the stranger's long lean body and the way his butt flexed in tight-fitting jeans. *Yum. So hot.*

He was roughly the same height as Drake, say six-one or two. Taller than I in my high heels. His loose-hipped walk, the set of his wide shoulders, the relaxed way he spoke to Drake, a man who intimidated many, all revealed that imitable male confidence that made good sense disengage from my brain.

Knowing they would eventually come to our table, I waited expectantly, hyperaware of my posture, my clothing, even the placement of my feet.

Heel touching instep, an inner voice reminded me. The pageant pose that was the most flattering,

They turned our way and I saw the stranger more clearly. His dress was similar to Drake's, who, thanks to a personal shopper, was always well put together. Starched and creased denim hugged his thighs. The hems of his jeans gathered just right over the shafts of cowboy boots. He wore a silver Western-style belt buckle and a long-sleeve button-down shirt the color of sunlight. It fit him so perfectly it could only be custom-made.

That package was more apt to catch my attention than a Brooks Brothers suit. Growing up around cowboys, I recognized a real one when I saw him. If this stranger wasn't one, he certainly knew how to dress like one.

Gabe's voice projected across the lobby as he strode toward them. "Drake. My man."

I watched as Drake introduced Gabe and the stranger, then they shook hands. The three of them talked. All that clearly came into my hearing range were deep huh-huh-huhs as they laughed together. Man-talk, fueled by testosterone. No women allowed. Typical alpha Type-As, all three of them.

I knew the type from first-hand experience. Not only was I unmercifully attracted to it, I'd had an on and off relationship with it for two years. I had even thought I wanted a permanent attachment until I made a stark discovery: I was committed, but my intended was still dating. I called that period of my life the second time I was lost in an asylum.

The trio broke apart and came to our table continuing their conversation about the Dallas Cowboys' loss last Sunday. Their absorption with football gave me a chance to study the Adonis who had tripped most of my triggers. He had classic facial features—chiseled nose, lean cheeks and square jaws. A sculptor's dream. The irises of his eyes were so brown they were almost black and they were framed by lashes so thick and black they looked as if he were wearing mascara.

His dark brown hair touched his collar. It was thick with a bit of a curl that appeared to be controlled by a good cut. Slightly sun-streaked, it looked clean and natural and un-saturated with hair product. You could run your fingers through it without worrying about damaging it. He was *sooo* good-looking.

Greek god, my inner voice said.

I couldn't stop staring, though I tried to be subtle.

All at once, he looked directly at me with a gaze so penetrating I felt as if he could see all the way through my clothing and the world tilted. An arcane force I couldn't identify, much less describe, captured me. Drake Lockhart had a *presence* that commanded a room, but this stranger exuded even more powerful vibes. Though I had never seen him before, I *knew* him. *Lead, follow or get out of my way.* That trope scrolled through my mind and stuck. I was a total sucker for men like him.

As if all of that wasn't enough to set off pandemonium within me, some instinct ingrained in my very core recognized a pure sexual energy rolling off him. A tingle darted through my sex and I shifted my feet to combat it. I had never been so carnally attracted to a man so instantly.

I had always thought it weird how one guy caused your hormones to riot and a dozen others didn't. Gabe, for instance. Good-looking and smart. I was sure he had a brilliant future. By any girl's standards, he was a good catch, but nothing about him roused my hormones or made a deep place low in my belly tighten as it was doing now.

The stranger was touched by me, too. I saw a flicker in those obsidian eyes. It had lasted for no more than a millisecond, but I was sure I wasn't mistaken. The very thought that he might be attracted to me caused heat to radiate through my system and warm even my cheeks.

Stop it! I was not ready for this hormonal assault. I had simplified my life. I had given up men and sex. At least until I got my feet back under me after Donald Sloan, the man who had used me, tried to change me and in the end, cheated on me.

I quickly looked down at the fliers stacked on the table.

Chapter 2

IF DRAKE NOTICED the sizzle between his friend and me, I couldn't tell. "Great party last night," he said to me. "My wife wants me to tell you she envied your dress."

I snapped out of the daze this stranger had put me in. My dress *was* enviable. Strategically adorned with crystal beads, it was a sleek black little number any fashion-conscious woman would adore. I had modeled it last year in Saks' Christmas show. After I gushed over it, the department store had given it to me instead of money.

I gave a silly titter. "Be sure to tell her I said thanks."

Drake turned to the stranger. "Tack, I need to talk to the concierge for a minute. This is Miranda March. She's assisting in the open house today. She'll escort you upstairs and show you around." He turned back to me. "Miranda, this is Harvey Tackett. He lives in Midland, but he needs a small pad to use when he's in the Metroplex on business."

Midland, Texas. Oil. And money.

"Ah, Midland," I managed to say with a smile, although my mouth had gone so dry my tongue felt thick. Willing my right hand not to tremble, I offered it.

Mr. Tackett's clearly defined lips eased into a hint of a smile that showed the edges of straight white teeth. His larger hand swallowed mine and a jolt vibrated my entire system.

"*Tack* Tackett," he said, with emphasis on "Tack," those dark chocolate eyes locked on my face. "My friends call me Tack."

His voice was deep, soft and raspy with only a hint of a Texas twang. The husky sound flowed through me like warm honey and again I thought of sex. I even felt a dampness in my panties. *Good Grief!* This was crazy.

Our gazes held and that sexual energy emanating from him grabbed me again. My thoughts scattered into a jumble that made my head swim for a few seconds. I mentally shook off the light-headedness. *He doesn't like his first name.* That was my first coherent thought after I recovered. Now I was disgusted with myself for reacting as if I were a teenybopper meeting Elvis.

"Be sure to show him the model on seventeen," Drake was saying. "Then go on up to the larger units on nineteen and twenty, okay?"

Being one of Drake's smaller developments, Skyline had only twenty floors. The smaller, more affordable units were below the sixteenth floor, "affordable" being a relative term. The "affordable" price in Skyline started at around two million. The units above the sixteenth floor, on the other hand, were all priced well past that. Just how far past was determined by the square footage and if a buyer requested "extras" beyond the ones that were already there. Obviously, Mr. Tack Tackett was no bargain shopper.

"Of course," I answered.

Drake had said "small" pad, but none of the units he suggested were small. I knew he had a big ego and I suspected he just wanted to show off his latest project to his friend. All I had to do was not let myself become distracted by a pretty face. After all, Mr. Tackett was just another guy, right? Better looking than most, but still, just another guy. Though he punched my hot buttons, he was probably no better than any man I knew or had known and he might be even worse.

Exactly, my inner voice agreed. *Good-looking men are never all they're cracked up to be.*

"Take notes, Tack. We'll talk later." Drake then turned to me. "Tack's a good friend of mine, Miranda, so take good care of him."

Ooh, yeah. With pleasure, that pesky inner voice chimed in.

Drake walked away, leaving Mr. Tackett in my care. I plucked a flier off the stack and passed it to my charge with a smile. "Ready?"

"When you are."

"Then follow me." I pulled my tablet from my bag and started for the elevators.

Tack Tackett's presence filled the small elevator car. Acute awareness of his size and masculinity had my heart tapping out a steady pitty-pat. When had I ever been in close quarters with a sexier guy?

Keep your cool and stay focused, my inner voice cautioned me.

Mr. Tackett's scent teased my nose. Clean, like fresh air and sun-dried laundry. Too subtle for cologne. Whatever it was, I loved it. I hadn't noticed it when he was standing with Drake and Gabe, both of whom wore exotic colognes.

The pricier units above the sixteenth floor were accessed only by a homeowner's key in a key slot in the control panel inside the elevators. I fumbled with the keys on the key ring, finally identified the master and plugged it in.

As the elevator car stirred into motion, I stepped back and stood against the sidewall. Mr. Tackett leaned against the back wall, his arms spread, his hands braced on the handrails. My gaze landed on his short well-kept nails and a heavy college ring. Texas A&M. An Aggie. I should have known. He fit the stereotype.

While his clothing had caught my attention in the beginning, one of his assets that had me tongue-tied and my hands sweating was his lean, flat-bellied body. From the corner of my eye, I homed in on his torso. Not an ounce of flab anywhere.

I knew the hours and discipline physical fitness required. I jogged or fast-walked several days a week, did yoga and cross fit when I could and sometimes I went to the gym and worked out with weights. I was in good shape. I was naturally drawn to men who were as fit as I was.

I simply couldn't keep from furtively ogling Mr. Tackett. My greedy eyes strayed from his midsection to his fly and that sexy little bump at the bottom of his zipper. From out of nowhere, curiosity sneaked up on me. Was he well-endowed?

Absolutely, that inner voice said inside my head.

I hadn't seen a real live naked man since Donald Sloan and I parted. I hadn't even seen pictures. I mentally undressed Mr. Tackett, imagined him with a rearing erection.

Careful. You're losing focus, that inner voice cautioned me.

Redirecting my attention, I searched for words to make conversation. "In town for long?"

Lame, pathetic and unoriginal, the voice complained.

"Just overnight."

"Great weather," I said.

"Yep."

Oh, my God. You're getting worse, that inner voice grumbled.

Mentally, I rolled my eyes.

We landed on the seventeenth floor and I led the way toward the first unit Drake had asked me to show and called up my routine pitch. "Several different models are available. All of them provide incomparable views. All offer the utmost privacy and security."

I omitted saying that all were finished out with what I considered to be obscene luxury. I was well aware that to the wealthy, no luxury seemed obscene.

I pointed up at a line of dark glass domes on the ceiling. "Security cameras. They work twenty-four-seven. Anything that happens in the hallway will be on film."

Mr. Tackett looked up. "And? How long before the cops show up?"

I stalled. "Um, I hate to admit it, but I don't have an answer to that question. But I'm sure the concierge does."

The unit we entered was a stylish two-bedroom, two-bath with traditional décor that I would love to own myself. It was perfect for a single woman. Or a single man. I leased a two-bedroom condo on the West Side. It wasn't a dump, but comparing it to the one I was showing Mr. Tackett at the moment was like comparing my small SUV to a Bentley.

He paged through the flier I had given him as I continued to point out the amenities—within walking distance of downtown and all that the dynamic Fort Worth downtown offered, walls of windows that overlooked the Trinity River and/or the City of Fort Worth, silk or bamboo wallpapers of the buyer's choice, beautiful nut-colored cabinetry and moldings throughout the living areas, floors of exotic hardwood and Italian marble, et cetera, et cetera, et cetera....

Having promoted everything from automobiles to rifles in various unconventional environments, I was as good at puffery as the next person, even when distracted. Thankfully, Skyline needed little puffery. The building and the condos sold themselves.

Mr. Tackett said little other than "Hm" and "I see."

As we took in the living and dining room areas, he glanced up at the hardwood beams in the coffered ceiling, then down at the matching hardwood floors.

"Drake doesn't like carpet," I explained, hoping my voice wasn't coming out shaky. "He installs it only in the bedrooms or by special request. You can choose carpet if you like, but it would be a crime to cover these beautiful floors."

"I've got no objection to wood floors," Mr. Tackett said.

Finally. A statement longer than three or four words.

"All of the units have artisan-type fireplaces with unique stone facades." I demonstrated how each could be ignited with the push of a button.

You are babbling like a loon, my inner voice said.

I know. I'm a nervous wreck, I replied. "Would you, um, like to see the kitchen?" I asked.

"Lead me to it."

We walked through a gourmet cook's kitchen. "This is every cook's dream. Top line appliances. No lack of built-in conveniences."

Mr. Tackett looked around, ran his long fingers along a glossy quartz countertop, "Nice. I cook sometimes."

The voice in my head perked up. *Ah-ha. No wife?*

The thought brought a smile to my lips.

"You won't have to unless you just want to. Once people start to move in, this will be a full-service building. A chef will be present downstairs twenty-four hours. You'll be able to have food delivered any time. It's part of the homeowners' package."

"Sweet. Housekeeping services?"

Find out if he has a wife, the ornery voice in my head persisted.

Why she was so demanding, I didn't know. I wasn't shopping for a husband or even a boyfriend. Well... Not *diligently* anyway.

"Laundry and dry cleaning if you want," I answered. "But on housekeeping, you're on your own. Or we can put you in touch with an agency."

We reached the master bedroom with ceilings as lofty as the living room's. Everything was off-white with splashes of pale beige and light blue. Earth and sky. Rustic oak furniture the color of driftwood blended with the color scheme. The air around us was redolent with a clean herbal scent. I barely resisted removing my shoes before walking onto the thick off-white carpet.

I had been in this room previously and a fantasy had already formed in my head—me moving around the room in a sexy white negligee, opening the blinds with the remote control and greeting the morning, gazing out over the river while I sipped at a cup of tea from a china cup that had been delivered by a personal maid. What would life be without a few fantasies?

"I love this room," I said. "It's so..."—I scrunched my shoulders and gave him a smile—"so comfortable."

Mr. Tackett looked over at the king-size bed that was covered by a pale blue and white duvet. He then swung his gaze to me and settled a look on me that was so dark and wicked it couldn't be anything other than an invitation. A case of nerves attacked me more aggressively. This was becoming ridiculous. I scrabbled for words that sounded professional. "Um, the furniture is from a local retailer. It can be purchased with the unit if you like."

One corner of his perfect mouth tipped up into a smile. Or was it a smirk? Could he read my mind? Did he know what he was doing to me? I quickly ducked my chin and made for the master bath, forcing him to follow me to keep up.

"Every bedroom has *en suite* facilities," I said. "And as you'll see, the master is to die for."

"*En suite*? That must be a real estate term."

I had heard it from Gabe. "It means a bathroom connected to the bedroom."

I walked around the huge room, yakking like a magpie. "The bathrooms in Drake's developments look like something from a magazine. Furniture-like vanities, the most up-to-date fixtures. Large walk-in closets and dressing rooms."

I gestured toward the closet area that adjoined one end of the bathroom and we walked into a space larger than my bedroom at my own condo. "As you can see, it has built-ins that match the other wood throughout the unit."

"I see."

He spent several minutes studying the finely crafted cabinetry. I stood by, shifting from one foot to the other to relieve the ache that had begun in my feet and ankles. Designer platform shoes with four-inch heels might look fantastic, but they were not ideal footwear for standing and walking all day.

Soon, he finished his inspection of the closet and dressing room and returned his attention to me. "What's next?"

I led him out to the bathing area at the opposite end of the room where a marble jet tub filled a corner. "Here, you have a jet tub large enough for two people to loll."

He stood there, his hands resting on his hips as he gazed down at the tub. Then he looked up and showered me with a smile that left me dazzled. "Looks like fun."

Fun? What did *that* mean?

Dummy. Fun. Get it?

I finally got it and a surge of heat squiggled all the way up to my cheeks. Evidently, his mind was on something besides the quality amenities. And it had been ever since we passed through the bedroom doorway. My own mind went blank. All that came to me was, "Um, here you also have heated towel bars and floor tiles."

He chuckled. "That's extravagant. When does it get cold enough around here for that to be important?"

My own opinion didn't count, but I happened to agree with him. In North Central Texas, freezing temperatures were the exception rather than the norm. I lifted my shoulders in a shrug. "It's a luxury add-on."

"But it's wasteful if it isn't needed. We shouldn't be wasteful just because we can."

Jeez! He might not say much, but when he spoke, he said a mouthful.

Now I was starting to think I needed to wind this up. A few feet from the tub, I opened a wide glass door to an oversized steam shower with so many controls it looked as if it could lift off at any moment. Mr. Tackett poked his head through the doorway and scanned floor, ceiling and walls thoroughly. "Hm. Interesting."

Interesting? A little frown tugged at my brow as I closed the shower door. When I turned around, he was only a couple of feet away. His appraising gaze slid down my front. Gooseflesh skittered over me. My nipples tightened and pushed against my camisole as if they were reaching toward him. Could he tell? Were they showing through my blouse? Men ogling me wasn't a new experience, but this extraordinary reaction by my body was totally unfamiliar. Was he having this effect on me because he was so damn good-looking? I pressed my tablet to my chest.

God, what would you do if you didn't have that tablet to hide behind? my inner voice grumbled.

"Would you like to move on?" I managed to ask.

I showed him four more units, including the one on the nineteenth floor that had four bedrooms and four baths spread over 4,000 square feet. All the while,

I talked a hundred miles an hour, concentrating on not letting my voice come out falsetto. He continued to say little.

I intended to end the tour on the twentieth floor in the largest unit where Gabe and I had been this morning. After a short trip on the elevator, we were at the private entrance. "This is one of four penthouse units," I said as I plugged the passkey into the front door lock. "We had the grand opening party here last night. I don't think I saw you."

"Wasn't in town last night. I flew in this morning."

Of course. No doubt he had a private plane. I arched my brow and lifted my chin knowingly. "Ah."

We scarcely got through the front door before Mr. Tackett checked his watch, a clunky black and gold thing that looked as if it were armed with whistles and bells. "Drake's probably finished by now," he said. "I don't want to make us late for our appointment."

"Oh. Let's go back downstairs then."

I had confused emotions. In a way, I was disappointed to part from his company. But the inner compass that guided me most of the time was glad for the escape. He was causing an edgy restlessness within me that had no room to thrive or even exist in my present life.

I led the way back to the elevator. The only way I was going to get through another ride in close quarters with this beautiful man without making an ass of myself was to keep talking. "On the lower floor, we have a well-equipped gym and a trainer available for someone who's interested. Also an area called the Office that's overseen by the concierge. It has a conference room, office machines and computers and a small post office that's staffed nine-to-five. It's across from the elevator. You'll see the sign when we get off."

Leaving the elevator, we passed up a tour of the gym and the Office and reached a large all-white space that was obviously a salon, though it wasn't yet open for business. "Here, besides a beauty salon, we'll have a spa that I'm sure your wife will appreciate."

He poked his head through the doorway and made a quick perusal of the space. "No wife."

That inner voice that had been badgering me pumped her fist. *Yes!*

Chapter 3

WE FOUND DRAKE waiting when we returned to the lobby. "What do you think?" he asked Tack.

Mr. Tackett nodded. "Nice."

Jeez, was that all he could say? The cheapest condo in this building was more than *nice.* Everyone who walked through any of the units oohed and aahed.

"Headed for the golf course?" Gabe asked Drake.

Drake grinned. "Not today. We're on our way to Weatherford. Tack's got an appointment to look at a horse. We're meeting my brother. He's the man who knows horses, but I'm going along to add my two-cents."

Ah. So he really is a cowboy. Then again, maybe not. No one knew better than a Texas country girl that owning a horse didn't make a guy a cowboy. But an appointment to look at a horse, accompanied by Drake's expert horseman brother, said the subject animal wasn't slated for the glue factory.

Cutting horse was my next thought. Owning cutting horses and having them trained to compete in various shows was a big, expensive hobby in Texas, and the cutting horse culture influenced many parts of Texas daily life. Nowadays, the value of a winning cutter exceeded the value of a Thoroughbred. With Fort Worth being the home of the National Cutting Horse Association, I both knew and ran into quite a few people who owned cutting horses. None of them were poor.

As Drake and Mr. Tackett started to leave, Mr. Tackett cast me a look over his shoulder that pierced all the way to my bone marrow and left me rattled. Still, I managed to lift my hand in a small wave.

Then they disappeared. I tingled all over. I needed a moment to recover from being in the company of a scrumptious man around whom the air crackled, even if he was a man of few words. I willed my attention to straightening the items on the table.

"Your face looks red," Gabe said. "You okay?"

With my fair complexion, "flushed" was how I usually looked when I was embarrassed or stressed. I had to get my aberrant thoughts and my blood pressure under control. "I'm fine. Guess it's the fast pace. We covered several units above the fifteenth floor pretty quickly."

"That dude's got your number," Gabe said. Obviously, he was not worried that my face looked red. "If looks could melt, you'd be a puddle on the floor about now. Exactly who is he?"

Gabe's comment did nothing to settle my nerves. I continued to fiddle with the flyers on the table. "You met him. He's a personal friend of Drake's."

"A personal friend, yeah, but who *is* he? Since he's from Midland, I'm guessing he's loaded. And he's a buyer, right? So Drake's going to keep him for himself."

If Harvey Tackett were not a personal friend, Drake would have already handed him off to Gabe. Since I wasn't a Realtor who would be collecting a commission, Drake asking me rather than Gabe to show the model assured that if Mr. Tackett bought, Drake would be able to retain the selling commission for his company. This was one of the reasons he hired me.

Gabe had to know this, but his tone dripped with resentment. I was sure he believed Drake should have given Mr. Tackett to him. The competition in real estate sales was fierce. Cutthroat even. Gabe was so hardline he had no qualm about going toe-to-toe with Drake over money. He had done it many times.

I knew nothing about the fine points of his and Drake's business arrangement and I didn't want to stick my nose into it. I finally looked up. "He's from West Texas," I said, hoping to change the subject.

"I'll bet he's in oil. Yep, he's loaded."

Gabe was worse than a dog with a bone, a trait that, no doubt, made him successful in sales. I had often wondered if he ever chilled out. *Give it a rest forgodsake*, I wanted to say, but I said instead. "Didn't he tell you what he did when y'all were having your *all-male tete-a-tete* over in the corner?"

"We were talking football."

"Well, there you go. You missed out on something important while your tongue was tied up by football." I gave him a saccharine smile.

Ignoring my sarcasm, he planted his fists on his slim hips, pushing back his jacket. "If he buys, I should get a piece of that action. I mean, after all, I'm here and you can't close him or write a contract, right?"

"Uh, no, I can't."

Just then, Michael Bolton's voice blared from inside my bag, allowing me to escape this conversation. I had downloaded *When a Man Loves a Woman* as a ringtone on my smartphone when I first met Donald Sloan. I didn't need a daily reminder of the tacky end of that relationship a year and a half ago, but the song was one of my favorites and I liked hearing it. I dug for the phone.

My twenty-two-year-old half-sister's name and picture appeared on the screen. *Crap! Now what?*

Lisa was six years younger than I and we were not phone buddies. She was twelve years old when I left my mother's house, so I really didn't know her very well as an adult. She called me only when she or our mother needed money or a crisis had erupted. Nothing could spoil my day more quickly than a phone call from either of them. Instantly, my good mood threatened to plummet.

"I need to take this," I told Gabe and walked toward the back of the lobby for privacy. "Hi, this is me."

"Mom quit taking those latest pills the doctor gave her."

As usual, Lisa hadn't even said hello before she started on her and our mother's issues. Mom was an alcoholic who suffered from bipolar disorder. Or if I wanted to be charitable, I could say she had always suffered from manic depression and eventually became an alcoholic. One affliction fed off the other.

As my thoughts veered to the possible result of her stopping the medication that leveled out her mood swings, my mouth quirked. "Why?"

"She thinks they're making her fat."

"I thought she was doing better with those pills. I hate to see her stop taking them. Maybe you should call the doctor and discuss it with him."

"And if he wants her to take something different, how's it gonna get paid for?"

I made a mental groan. I had spent the first eighteen years of my life managing and combating Mom's illness and its consequences. Now, I was ten years removed from that onus, but that didn't mean I was relieved of it. Mom had no money and her meds were expensive. I had hassled for months arranging for her to get free medication directly from the pharmaceutical company that made it. "At the moment, I don't know. I'd have to look into it."

In your spare time, right? my inner voice snarked. Unspoken sarcasm gave me the patience to deal with my little sister's ineptitude and my mother and her husbands.

I didn't want to worry about them today. Working in a PR job as I was doing, I needed to be bubbly and enthusiastic, not burdened by guilt and anger. But mentally, I was already withdrawing from the pleasant day to deal with the latest family crisis.

"I guess I might as well tell you," Lisa went on. "Arnie got arrested for shoplifting in Walgreens in Abilene. I had to go up there and get him out of jail. Then him and Mom got into this big fight and he left. Now she's all down and upset."

Arnold Hamlin. My mother's latest—and fifth—husband.

Crap! My jaw tightened. "She really needs to get back on that medication, Lisa. When did Arnie leave? Is it for good?"

"Yesterday. He'll probably come back today. I mean, where's he gonna go? Mom says she doesn't care if he stays gone, but she's been bawling ever since he left."

"What did he try to steal?"

"Cigarettes. They caught him behind the cash register putting 'em in his jacket pocket."

Shit! I was dumbfounded. A picture came to me of the last Walgreens I was in. "Walgreens has locked counters and security cameras," I said. "Unless you're a magician, getting into the cigarette display would be almost impossible. How did he get back there?"

"How would I know what he did, Miranda? I don't even know if that was the first time he ever did it."

My reflection in the marble wall showed my mouth turned down in a horseshoe scowl. I straightened my spine, turned in the opposite direction and heaved a loud sigh meant to be audible on the other end of the line.

"What am I supposed to do about it?" Lisa said defensively. "They put him in jail, Miranda. Somebody had to go get him out. He's not that bad. He's your stepfather, too, you know."

I had never considered Arnold Hamlin my stepfather or anything at all to me. He and my mother had been married roughly three years, so he hadn't been around when I still lived with her and Lisa.

I had mixed emotions about Arnie. At one time, he had made my mother happy, thus, he made me happy. But now, the honeymoon was over and they occupied the same cage. If you stayed around them long, you had to wonder which would devour the other first. He, too, was an alcoholic who had spent more time and energy in a quest to get disability benefits from Social Security than he had ever spent on a job. Other than being a drunk, he had no visible disability.

A part of me felt guilty for the fraud he perpetrated daily. But another part was grateful he was getting money from somewhere besides me. I should report him, but I hadn't even looked into how I would do it. I felt guilty about that, too.

I paced toward the fire exit. "He's a fifty-five-year-old man who's been a jerk for as long as I've known him. Nothing I hear about him comes as a surprise. Good grief, Lisa, who's dumb enough to go behind the counter at a Walgreens and steal cigarettes? Do you think rescuing him was worth the cost?"

I sensed Lisa's growing frustration and I didn't have to wait long to hear the real reason for her call. "Listen, did you send us a check? It wasn't in yesterday's mail."

The U.S. Government, the great State of Texas and I provided the livelihoods for this trio. The government supplied monthly checks, Medicaid and a Lone Star card. I carried out my part by working Monday through Thursday nights as a bartender at Smoky Joe's, a neighborhood cocktail lounge not far from where I lived.

I had learned to tend bar while I was still a student and so far, that knowledge had served me as well as what I had learned in college. I sent most of my earnings from Smoky's to Mom and Lisa. I had done this at first to avoid taking money out of my fledgling business. Gala was profitable now, but I still wasn't confident enough to give up my bartending job. The cocktail lounge was upscale and I did well on tips. Usually, it was enough.

"I haven't gotten around to sending it yet. I'm working all weekend."

I had blocked out the entire weekend for this gig with Lockhart Concepts and I normally wouldn't even be thinking about anything else. Drake Lockhart paid me well and I gave his events my undivided attention.

"Oh," Lisa said.

The disappointment in her reply was impossible to ignore. "Why are your finances in such an urgent state all of a sudden? I sent you money last week."

Thinking of the four nights of four-to-midnight on my feet at Smoky's, I did a one-eighty and paced in the opposite direction.

"It took all of that to get Dad out."

Dad? Besides hating that Lisa had spent the money I had worked for on getting Husband #5 out of jail, I hated hearing her call him "Dad." "You shouldn't call Arnie 'Dad,' Lisa. He isn't your father."

"It's just easier, Miranda. You don't live here, so you don't know."

My sister was no more acquainted with her natural father than I was with mine. If she needed to call Arnie "Dad," so be it. I said no more.

But at least her father is somewhere out there and he and Mom were married when she was born, my irritated inner voice reminded me.

"Mom's been so down since her and Arnie had that big fight," Lisa went on. "I'm scared she'll get into one of those moods where she starts talking about killing herself."

Oh, hell. My mother had never attempted suicide, but until she started the meds she had just stopped taking, she had talked about it, which was scary enough. A trip to West Texas loomed in my immediate future.

"I was gonna use the money to put gas in the car and take her out to eat," Lisa said. "Maybe go to a movie."

I couldn't help but think of all the times I *hadn't* gone out to eat or gone to the movies because I was always working. Now I was feeling pissy, spoiling for a fight. Miranda the Cynic rose to the occasion. "What, restaurants stopped taking Lone Star cards?"

Lisa didn't take the bait. Maybe she didn't even recognize the derision. "Mom maxed out that card," she said. "She found a sale on Dr. Pepper up in Abilene and used the card to buy all of it. You know how she is about Dr. Pepper. Now we've got cases of that shit all over the house. I told that state counselor the way Mom is, trying to get her to add money to the card, but she wouldn't."

The more Lisa talked, the clearer it became that our mother had been—or maybe continued to be—in a manic episode. Anything might happen next. "Please tell me that Dr. Pepper is all she's drinking."

"She spikes it with a little vodka, but I'm keeping an eye on the bottle. I marked it with a Sharpie."

I rolled my eyes.

"Anyway, we've all been stuck here in this old house, Miranda. We need a change of scenery. Could you send a little extra?"

As I thought about all that Lisa had told me, I also had to consider that I never knew what to believe when she or Mom asked me for extra money. Mom had told me fibs my entire life because that was just what she did. Fabrications and exaggerations were part of her illness. One of my most vivid childhood memories was when she had come to an elementary school party dressed like Norma Desmond from *Sunset Boulevard*. My classmates had thought she was cool. At the time, I had thought so, too, but later, after I was older, I realized how far out there Mom had been that day and that my teacher had been horrified.

Yep, no one could embellish a story like my mother could. Lisa, on the other hand, was a liar of convenience.

A tic began to twitch in my right eye. I walked back toward the entrance. "I don't know, Lisa. I'll have to see how much I've got to spare. Like I said, it'll be Monday before I get it in the mail, okay? If you're that desperate, maybe you can return some of the Dr. Pepper for a refund."

"Well, duh-uh. I have to be able to drive the car to do that. And the gas tank's empty, remember?"

I wanted to curl up in a corner and howl. Then, I glimpsed Gabe and the two cops Drake had hired as security striding toward the front door. Gabe was ready to open for business. "I need to go," I said quickly. "I'm working."

I disconnected before Lisa could say anything else. More words were unnecessary. We had covered the reason for her call. I had a too-vivid picture of the situation. As soon as this Skyline weekend was over, I had to get to West Texas.

I quickstepped back to the table and shoved my phone back into my bag. Calling up my game face, I scrabbled for an upbeat attitude. Life with my mother hadn't done much for me, but it had trained me to be an expert at quick recovery.

"Everything okay?" Gabe asked as I caught up with him.

"No problem. Just my little sister keeping me tuned in to what the family's up to."

Through the afternoon, we were busy. We showed the condo units and the building to dozens of people, but my mind was never on what I was doing. Lisa, my mother and Harvey Tackett all bounced around inside my head, each one vying for my attention. I already knew what I had to do about Mom and Lisa, but Mr. Tackett was a sexy, intriguing daydream. I couldn't erase the vision of his long, lean body without clothes. Was it as solid and chiseled as it looked? What might sex with him be like?

Every time my thoughts ventured into that erotic territory, my inner voice nagged me. *You've lost your mind. You'll never see him again....You know what? You've gone without for too long....You need to find a boyfriend.*

But I'm too busy for a boyfriend, I argued. *What's wrong with fantasizing?*

The open house was planned to end at six. By five, traffic had dwindled to nothing. Gabe was feverishly texting with someone and stalking around as if he had ants in his pants. Having written two sales contracts that totaled five million dollars, he was stoked. If both deals closed, his commissions and bonuses would be enormous. He tried to put up a gallant front, but I could tell he could hardly wait to escape. He probably intended to celebrate his profitable day with a hot date.

Part of me envied him. Not only the money he made, but the social life he had. I hadn't had a Saturday night date in months. Since the breakup with Donald, I had channeled most of my time and energy into Gala. The extra effort had resulted in a workload that was almost too much for one person. Having only a part-time assistant, I worked almost every weekend nowadays. When I wasn't working, I spent Saturday nights letting down with a book or blanking out in front of TV.

And when loneliness and yearning got the best of me, sometimes, in the dark of my bedroom, I called on BOB, my battery-operated boyfriend. The gel device had been a gift from my friends.

I had graduated from high school in Roundup, Texas, a virgin. In school, I'd had almost no friends and I hadn't once had a boyfriend. With Mom's mood swings and unpredictable behavior, made more so by alcohol and various men passing through as if our house had a revolving door, life had been way too complicated for simple social activities like girlfriends, boyfriends and dates. Not that I had never been invited on a date, but to have gone would have been more than I could have managed back then.

I could sing. And in my isolation and as an escape, I had taught myself to play an old guitar that had belonged to my grandpa. My grandmother was convinced that I was another Carrie Underwood. With her help, I entered the contest for Miss Roundup. No one was more amazed than I when I won, singing a country song.

My grandmother had been beyond excited. She bought me a new guitar and pushed me to go on to Miss Redfield County, then a tri-county contest and finally, I became a contestant in the Miss Texas pageant. I didn't win in that one, but I became a finalist. I received money and a partial college scholarship. A new world opened to me and a goal took root in my psyche.

As soon as I graduated from high school, I moved to Fort Worth, got a job and made entering beauty pageants a mission. With numerous pageants behind me and enough money to start college, I enrolled. Oddly enough, I never once entertained the notion that I would become a professional singer. The prize I had my eye on was a college degree.

My newfound girlfriends in Fort Worth had soon learned that I was "socially underdeveloped" and spent untold hours and energy trying to fix me up with the right boy to deflower me. They failed. I found someone on my own, which had turned out to be a disappointment as well as a colossal mistake and turned me off of sex for quite a while.

My misadventures with boys, or young men, became a joke among my girlfriends and me. As a gag gift for my twenty-first birthday, they had pooled their money and bought me BOB.

Since those days, that sex toy had taken the edge off more than once during the long dry spells that were my life. And BOB had found a place inside me that not one of my former sex partners had ever touched or even attempted to find. I had begun to wonder if most men even knew where and what it was. I wasn't sure myself, although I had done some scant research on YouTube and Wikipedia.

I was facing an idle evening, so I said to Gabe, "If you want to leave early, I'll hang in here until six. If a buyer shows up, I can call you."

He thanked me and rushed away.

Outside, the day was waning. My feet were numb and my ankles felt as if they were broken. I was in the mood to sue some shoe designer.

At 6:30, Paul, the concierge, dismissed the two cops who had stayed with us all day. After I killed the elevator music coming from the sound system, I found him at his desk in his office. "I'm ready to go home. Is someone supposed to go upstairs and lock everything?"

He looked up at me through thick lenses in his black-framed glasses. "Can you do it? I've still got to get some things done here and I need to get home. Some of my wife's relatives are in town for the weekend."

Crap. My intent had been to remind him, not volunteer to take on the chore myself. With dark coming on, I didn't relish going back upstairs alone, but saying that to Paul might sound like whining. I wished he hadn't already sent those cops on their way. With a mental sigh, I steeled myself for the task I was pegged to do. "Watch the elevators and be sure no one comes up behind me, okay?"

"Will do, Miss March."

His reply made me want to grind my teeth. I hated when someone called me Miss March.

He made no attempt to leave his desk.

Resigned, I started for the elevators. I hadn't taken three steps before, to my astonishment, Tack Tackett walked through the glass entryway. My heart slammed against my ribs.

What the hell?...Had he forgotten something? I glanced around.

He walked straight toward me, those mysterious midnight eyes piercing me, his lips tipped up with that sexy one-sided smile. That scent that had lured me earlier in the elevator filled the air around me.

"You're still here. I was afraid you'd be gone by now."

He had come back to see *me*? *Oh. My. God.* My brain froze and I had to work to give an intelligible reply. "Uh, not yet, but... Well, the open house is over. I'm, uh...just going upstairs to lock up."

"Alone?"

"Well....Yes," I said at last.

"You shouldn't do that alone. I'll go with you. I'd like a second look anyway."

I hesitated, gathering my wits. Apart from the personal safety issue, I reminded myself that I was holding two passkeys—one that gave me entry to every unit on the fifteenth floor and below and another that got me into every unit above. The pricier models had antique furnishings, Aubusson rugs on the floors, original art on the walls, one-of-a-kind bronze statuary, porcelain vases on tables here and there and other miscellaneous objects that might attract a thief. Unless accompanied by Gabe, the concierge or me, no one had been allowed alone upstairs all-day.

Oh, stop it, my inner voice grumbled. *Didn't Drake say he's a good friend?*

I was glad to have someone go with me. And Mr. Tackett had a dragon-slayer air about him that made me think I could trust him. So, I said, "Okay, then. Let's go.

Chapter 4

As we waited for the elevators, the fact that everything between Mr. Harvey Tackett and me had changed sank in. He was no longer an every woman's unbelievably studly guy that I would never see again. He was now a sexy, good-looking predator who had returned to Skyline on the hunt. And the prey was me. My heart began to flutter.

As the elevator doors glided closed, I leaned against the back wall, a death grip on the key ring. Making conversation was a dozen times more difficult than earlier. In the confines of the elevator car, my pulse sounded in my ears so loudly I could hear it. I wouldn't have been surprised if *he* could hear it. Or if he had already read my thoughts and sensed the sexual tension that had me tied in knots. Maybe my inner voice was right. Maybe I had gone without too long. I drew a calming breath and willed myself to not squirm.

He, on the other hand, seemed to be relaxed. An I-can-kick-any-dragon's-ass confidence exuded from him.

"Drake tells me you're not married," he said.

That inner voice that thought I needed help piped up. *Boo! Hiss! Not appropriate.*

Stifling a gasp, I stiffened. My relationship with Drake Lockhart was strictly professional. Why would he discuss me personally with someone? Should I be angry that apparently he had done just that? We landed on the sixth floor before I found my voice. "Um, no. I'm not."

He gestured me out of the elevator ahead of himself. I strode at a clip toward a unit I had shown a young couple earlier. He kept up, matching my stride. "Are we in a race?"

I dared not let myself look at him. "I have to check several units and I'd like to get home. It's been a long day. My feet are killing me."

From the corner of my eye, I glimpsed him looking down at my feet. "Wrong shoes," he muttered.

I chose not to reply.

At the small unit's front door, I unlocked it and we stepped inside. "Feel free to look around. This will take me only a minute."

"I'm in no hurry. You're the one in a rush."

I left him in the living room gazing out at the view of the city, his hands shoved into his jeans pockets, again revealing his flat stomach, which did nothing to cool the stew simmering within me. I sailed through each of the rooms, double-checking the closets and making sure all was well and hoping I didn't miss anything. I was so distracted by him and what the situation between us had suddenly become.

In the master bathroom, I stopped and checked my makeup and hair in the vanity mirror. My lipstick had faded. My long auburn hair that I had pulled back in a ponytail and clipped with a gold barrette was disorderly. Wispy strands had come loose around my face. I had not a single tool. I could do nothing about either the lipstick or the hair.

When I returned to the living room, he still stood in front of the window wall where I had left him. I called up a phony smile. "The view is great, isn't it?"

"Sure is." He gave me a look across his shoulder, his eyelids narrowed into a squint. "Does Drake know you come up here alone?"

What?...

Drake and I had never discussed that issue. I skidded back into my quick recovery mode and gave a nervous titter. "I can't imagine Drake accepting I-was-afraid-to-go-upstairs-alone as an excuse for leaving all the doors unlocked. I asked the concierge to watch the elevators and not let anyone else come up behind me."

Why I was making a speech about this I didn't know. It was none of Mr. Tackett's business.

His brow furrowed and he gave me a how-can-you-be-so dumb look. "Trust me. That guy never left his office."

Exactly what *I* thought, but I didn't want to say it and make myself sound wimpy.

"You're a pretty woman," he said. "There's more to think about than somebody following you. An empty building like this? Some nut could hang out all day, waiting for an opportunity. If you worked for me, I wouldn't expect you to take chances like this."

Now he had put words to one of my own concerns, making me nervous for a different reason. "If I dwelled on the negative possibilities, I might scare myself. Please. Don't plant evil thoughts in my mind."

"The concierge should be the one to lock the doors. Or those cops. Or the dude who was here with you this afternoon. One of them should have volunteered to do it. What's wrong with them?"

His provincial attitude caught me off-guard, but at the same time, someone like him showing concern for my safety hooked me in a subtle way. I released a small sigh. "Look, I understand what you're saying, but it's okay. Really. I'm doing just fine. I hope you aren't going to mention it to Drake."

"Somebody should. I'm surprised he hasn't thought of it."

"I'm expecting to see him tomorrow and I'll say something to him, okay?"

His jaw flexed. He wasn't satisfied with that answer. No doubt he *would* take it up with Drake. *Good grief!*

"Have you got a boyfriend?"

Oh, my God, that voice in my head shrieked. *Tell him that is none of his business.... No, wait. Don't scare him away. Just tell him no....*

That voice that was usually so confident it was right couldn't make up its mind.

Despite my muddle-headedness, an indefinable emotion squiggled through me. I stalled answering. I didn't want this Adonis to know I hadn't had a boyfriend in way more than a year. Or that I hadn't even had a date in months. I didn't want him to think I was chopped liver.

"Well, do you? One that you're sleeping with?"

Whoa! I blinked. Telling a stranger whether I have "a boyfriend" was one thing. Discussing with whom I might or might not be sleeping was another. I floundered for words. Finally, I hiked my nose in the air and managed to show indignation I wasn't sure I felt. "Mr. Tackett, Drake Lockhart and I are business associates. I don't discuss my private life with his friends. Or with his customers."

One corner of his etched lips tilted up in that smirk that had become familiar. Frustrated, I turned and stamped toward the front door, hoping I didn't stumble in my "wrong shoes." And as I went, I felt the burn of his stare on my bottom and that caused all sorts of contortions in my midsection.

He caught up with me. We traversed the hallway back to the elevator and re-boarded. While I checked four more units, he tagged along making clever comments about Skyline's various features, as if he were trying to make up for possibly annoying me.

That inner voice piped up again. *He not only looks like a god, he might have a personality.*

We rode to the seventeenth floor and the small unit I had shown him this morning. If Drake had wanted me to show this one to him in the first place, he must have thought he might buy it, so letting him see it a second time couldn't be a bad thing, right?

"Go ahead and take a second look around," I told him. "I'm going to check the other rooms for spooks and dead bodies."

"Yell at me if you find any." He chuckled, a deep masculine heh-heh-heh that sounded almost intimate.

I left him looking around the living room. Once I was out of his sight, I released the breath I had been holding. My midsection was tight and trembling. I had been moving so fast my pulse rate had kicked up as if I had been jogging and I felt damp all over. I finished my inspection of all four bedrooms and closets, unable to stop thinking and wondering about him. I had about a million questions.

By the time we reached the 6,000-square-foot unit on the twentieth floor where Gabe and I had met this morning, a peculiar connection had developed between Mr. Tackett and me. It was indefinable and it implied more than the facts. I didn't understand it.

I unlocked the door and preceded him as we walked into one of Skyline's premiere units located on the east side of the building. Due to the fading sunlight, the place was cast in dim golden light and dramatic shadows. I had wanted to get back downstairs before dark, but we hadn't quite succeeded. I pressed on the indirect lighting that presented the rooms in a more evocative ambience.

"Since we cut our tour short this morning, we didn't go through this unit," I said. "Would you like to see something breathtaking?"

His eyes lit up and he smiled. "More breathtaking than you?"

Now that's corny, that pesky inner voice groused.

I agreed, but a guy as sexy and good-looking as Mr. Tackett could get by with being trite. Instead of attempting a cute response, I said, "Come this way."

I walked him over to the window wall and the 180-degree view of the outside. Until last night's cocktail party, I hadn't been up here after dark. The evening view of the city lights winking and twinkling to life was even more dramatic than the daytime vista. Standing side by side, shoulders almost touching, we remained silent and gave the scene the admiration it deserved.

Finally, I said, "This is stunning, isn't it? It's like standing on a cloud above the city."

He walked right up to where his boot toes almost touched the glass and looked down. I didn't have the nerve to do this. If I went within a foot of the windows, I got dizzy and a fear of the glass breaking threatened to overwhelm me, though Drake had told me it would take a freight train to break the glass.

"Too bad I need only a small space," Mr. Tackett said. "This is tempting."

Tempting? If it was tempting enough, he would have to shell out twelve million dollars. Or close to it even if Drake was willing to negotiate. Just how rich was Mr. Tackett?

Being unlicensed, I wasn't allowed to quote specific prices, but I could get by with generalizing. "In New York City, this much space and luxury in a high-rise would cost you quite a lot more."

Why I chose that as a comparison, I didn't know. I knew nothing about New York City real estate. I had been there one time in my life and the Big Apple and Cowtown were like two different countries. My synapses truly must be fried.

He turned toward me, his hands shoved into his pockets. "And in Midland, Texas, it would cost me a lot less. If it existed."

Our faces were a foot apart, close enough to overload every one of my senses. His gaze flicked over my face, then settled on my eyes. "You've got the prettiest eyes. Somebody must tell you that every day."

My whole system started to churn and my cheeks warmed. I ducked my chin and drew a deep breath, causing my chest to noticeably rise and fall. "Th— Thank you. It's, um, unusual for someone with my hair color to have blue eyes."

Useless information. Dear God, I'm stammering. What was wrong with me? People *had* often told me I have pretty eyes and I usually said "thank you" and moved on.

The corners of his mouth tipped into that elusive smile that almost wasn't. "Yes, ma'am, they're blue all right. Blue as the Texas sky."

His voice had become a purr. That and staring at his perfectly-formed lips had me paralyzed. *My. God. This is surreal.* My own mouth quirked into a quick smile that came and went.

"Is your hair really that color?"

Fighting the urge to touch my hair, I gave a cajoling tsk-tsk. "Seriously? You're asking a woman you don't know if she dyes her hair?"

One wide shoulder lifted in a shrug. His eyes held mine for a few more beats. Even as dark as his irises were, I saw the heat of passion and it affected me dramatically, as if he were touching me in a forbidden place.

"I like red hair," he said. "If it's natural, I like it even more." He gave me another one-sided smile.

"And for what it's worth, I'm having a hard time convincing myself that I don't know you."

Oh, hell! Is this flirting? What went on between Gabe and me was flirting. Harmless. It had never lured me the way this beautiful stranger's soft words were enticing me now. I couldn't attach a name to what was happening, but this was more than playing. And I couldn't think of a single smart comeback. "I—I, well, really...No, um...I don't dye it."

He didn't reply. Just grasped my upper arm, leaned in and tenderly kissed one side of my upper lip.

I nearly stopped breathing. My eyelids drifted shut. His mouth lifted and kissed the other side, then gently bit my lower lip. When he stopped, my eyes fluttered open. His ardent black eyes held me stone still. His breath touched my lips, its minty scent reaching my nostrils. My heart raced around my rib cage as if it were a trapped hamster.

"Miranda," he murmured, as if his tongue were testing the name. "Pretty name for a pretty woman."

His strong arms came around my waist and pulled me close, his head angled in the opposite direction and his mouth covered mine.

All of the craving that had been harrying me all day, the tension and confusion and even lust that I had been fighting sprang up and traveled to parts below and I wanted *everything*. With him.

His tongue nudged my lips. I tentatively parted them and that was all the encouragement he needed. His hand cupped my jaw, held it firmly while he took possession of my mouth with gentle suction and long, lush licks and an erotic skill I had never experienced. His male scent and the warmth of his body engulfed me. My nipples hardened. A contraction squeezed deep in my sex. An unfamiliar world of wanting and needing spun around me and I was lost.

Instinctively, my arm slid around his thick shoulder and I kissed him back like for like.

I felt rather than heard a low groan rumble up from deep in his throat. The keys I held slipped from my hand and hit the floor and I combed my freed fingers into the back of his silky hair as we continued to ravage each other's mouths.

His hands traveled down and clutched my bottom, pressed my pelvis fully against an erection that felt like a steel bar. The visual I'd had of him in the elevator—his penis naked, hard and huge—took over my mind and a tingle so sweet and sharp it was almost more than I could bear darted to the core of my sex. No kiss had ever seduced me so completely.

His hand left my bottom and his fingers moved up, pulled my blouse tail free of my skirt's waistband. He drew back, his breathing shuddery as the two of us watched himself expertly unhook my blouse buttons and brush the panels of silk fabric aside. My own breath was coming in quick pants I tried not to show.

He smoothed his hand over my braless breasts that were flattened by the tight Spandex lace of my cami. When he couldn't take one in hand, he looked down at my torso. "Jesus, what *is* this thing?"

I fought an urge to grab the cami's hem, yank the shielding garment over my head and bare my chest.

He gave up on the camisole and circled my firm nipple with his palm, ducked his head and moved his mouth down, radiating damp warmth around my nipple through the tight fabric and somehow he succeeded in tonguing it and sucking. My sex answered with deep contractions and my body instinctively arched to the pleasure. I couldn't hold back a great sigh.

His mouth dragged away from my breast and trailed upward again to the bare skin above the camisole's lace edge, over the slopes of my breasts and on up, all the way to the hollow of my throat, his tongue tasting the elevated pulse point. He moved on over to where my neck joined my shoulder. He licked, then sucked, then soothed with another lick. I tilted my head, savoring his warm mouth on my throat and neck. He nuzzled below my ear, gently closed his teeth on my earlobe and tugged.

"I want to fuck you, Miranda," he said softly.

Omigod! A new shot of adrenaline rocketed through my body. I should have been insulted by such a crude declaration coming from a total stranger, but for a reason I couldn't explain even to myself, I wasn't.

Instead, I was dangerously close to thinking he had presented a great idea.

Though no man had ever talked dirty to me, something my hairdresser, Ashley Harrison, said to me once barged into my mind: *Honey, there ain't no bigger turn-on than when some guy just flat out tells you he wants to fuck you.*

Oh. My. God. She was so right.

And to prove it, my better judgment was going under for the third time in a dark pool of desire. My knees were quaking, my sex was tingling and it felt so good I didn't want to stop it.

But I had to.

My survival instinct buoyed me back to the surface. I pushed against his chest, leaned back against his arm and stared into black eyes that gave away nothing. "You're taking a lot for granted," I said, my words coming out choppy. "I don't know what Drake has told you or what you're reading into—"

"Stop right there." Instantly, he released me, stepped back and away from me, his breathing harsh.

Bereft, I stared at him.

Jamming his fists against his hips, he glared back at me. "You don't strike me as a naïve woman, so don't try to make me think you are one."

Oh, wow. If he only knew. My experiences with sex ranged from disappointing to downright awkward, up to and including Donald Sloan, the man I had slept with on and off for two years, the man I had thought at one point I wanted to marry and the man who knew less about sex than I did. What I thought were the facts about sex, I had heard from girlfriends or read in *Cosmo.*

I huffed, trying to show irritation equal to his, though what I felt was anything but irritation. "I'm not trying to make you think anything at all."

His dark eyes glowered. "You think Drake and I share locker room stories? Like a couple of teenagers?"

I couldn't imagine the sophisticated Drake Lockhart doing such a thing. Feeling silly, I turned my head and rubbed my hand up and down my opposite arm. "Of course not."

But refusing to look at him didn't resolve my dilemma. Somehow, for the sake of my own self-respect and my continued good reputation with Lockhart Concepts, I had to put things back on an even keel. Yet, as surely as my common sense knew that was what I needed to do, another part of me was ridiculously excited by his making what he wanted with me unabashedly clear.

"I'm not a game player, Miranda. I don't have time for it. You've got the same itch as me. I can tell. We're two grown people. So, baby, let's don't waste time."

Oh, God. Did he know where my head had been all-day? Such frankness was as intimidating as it was arousing, but I had to brake this runaway train. I had to stop him and myself both. With a deep, but unsteady breath, I faced him. "Listen, I don't do recreational sex. I just don't."

He tilted his head to the right, his eyes squinted. "Why?"

Oh, hell. I was losing ground. Now, not only was I ready to ignite and so wet that my inner thighs and the lacy tops of my thigh-high stockings were slick, I was on the verge of panic. "It's risky and demeaning. And unsatisfying." To my own ears, my voice sounded as if I were barking in a well.

"Then you've hooked up with the wrong partners. I'll make sure you don't feel that way. And you won't go away unsatisfied. That, I promise you."

He said that matter-of-factly in that raspy, devastating voice. Oh, he could deliver on that promise all right. I had not one shred of doubt. But how could we be having this intimate conversation so casually when we scarcely knew each other? And I cringed at the expression "hooked up." It reminded me too much of the episode after which I truly had given up recreational sex.

"You know what? I've always hated that expression, *hook-up*. It sounds like dogs in heat. I don't expect a lifetime commitment, but to me, sex has to have some meaning."

"I hear you. It's better to engage on more than one level." His posture relaxed and he opened his palms. "Look, Miranda, I'd love to ply you with wine and smother you with roses. But as it is, I'm short on time. I've got to be back in Midland tomorrow." He planted his hands on his hips again and gave me that smirky grin and a wink. "But I do have time to make you come a dozen times."

Oh. My. God, my inner voice exclaimed. *That is so not cute. Could he be any more obnoxious? What are you going to do?*

My immediate inclination was to roast him with a caustic remark, stalk off and leave him standing, but I couldn't do that without creating an incident. He and I were the only people on the twentieth floor of a high-rise building and I was the person with all the keys. Was I going to walk off and leave him here? No, I wasn't. If I ever wanted to work for Lockhart Concepts again, I could *not* anger or embarrass one of the CEO's friends and customers. But how could I tactfully make him understand that sex with me was not part of the deal on a condo in Skyline?

Beyond all of that, in my limited experience, more than half the time, I had never come at all. A dozen times wasn't even possible....*Was it?*

Stepping sideways, I put space between us, squatted and picked up the keys I had dropped. "Listen, we should *not* be here doing this. I apologize for letting it happen. I need to lock up everything and get back downstairs. I'm sure Paul's wondering why I'm taking so long."

He bent, put his hand under my elbow and effortlessly stood me on my feet. "Who's Paul, that concierge? That guy hasn't given two thoughts to what you might be doing."

His arm came around my waist and his black eyes captured mine. "Miranda. Since the minute I saw you this morning, getting you under me is all I've been able to think about. I haven't felt that urge that strong in a helluva long time." He bent down and tenderly nipped my lower lip. "Let me make love to you."

He might as well have thrown kerosene on a fire. Hearing that voice across a pillow sailed into my imagination. When I didn't reply, he pulled me closer and his mouth took mine in another demanding kiss and I didn't resist.

Well, making love is different from fucking, my inner voice told me smugly.

Chapter 5

BEFORE I HAD time to wonder what might happen next, Mr. Tackett and I were half-sitting, half-lying against the dozen or so coordinated designer pillows on the living room sofa and I was confined between his big body and the sofa back. My thighs were draped over his and we were kissing like hormone-driven teenagers in the backseat at Lover's Leap. Did he plan for us to do it on this sofa? I recoiled at the thought. I didn't know how much the sofa cost, but I was fairly certain the price tag was in the high five-digit range.

His hand came behind my neck. "I want to see your hair."

"No, don't—"

But he had already released my barrette, freeing my long, thick hair. He brought strands of it around my shoulders and fingered them, smiling down at me. "I love your hair."

He cupped my neck with a large hand and kissed me again, then trailed his opposite hand down my torso, over my hip, down my leg all the way to my feet. He slipped off my shoes, sat up and began massaging my foot and ankle with strong hands and fingers. *Good grief!*

"I don't know why women torture themselves with shoes like these."

The only male who had touched my feet and legs in months was Tran Rung whom I paid for pedicures. I closed my eyes and savored the massage. "Mmm, that feels *sooo* good.

He moved to the other foot. "Better now?"

I stretched my foot and arched it in his hand. "Ooh, yes...."

He ran his fingernail up my arch and sensation pricked deep in my sex. My foot jerked and my eyelids sprang open. "Oh..."

He looked back and over his shoulder at me. "Right connection?"

I didn't dare answer.

He lay back beside me and gave me a quick chaste kiss. The corners of his mouth turned up in a smile. "You've got the most kissable lips."

Then, his hand was on my knee, easing up the inside of my leg and under the hem of my skirt, leaving goosebumps in its wake. My heartbeat stuttered, but I made not a peep of protest. Oh, he was very smooth.

I was so aroused I wanted to part my legs to give him access to more, but I hadn't quite come to terms with what was happening or with my own emotions. And I was embarrassed that the insides of my thighs and the tops of my stockings were damp.

He broke the kiss when his hand reached the lacy elastic of my stocking tops. He gave a little frown. "What're you wearing?"

"Don't tell me you've never heard of thigh-high stockings."

He pushed my hem up, all the way to my crotch, his gaze following his fingers.

The potent scent of my arousal bloomed around us. No way could he not know why my thighs and stockings were wet. My cheeks flamed. *Dear God.* What would he think? I clutched his hand, stopping him and pressed my thighs together. I twisted my face away.

"It's normal, baby. Don't be embarrassed. Not with me." His voice had become even softer and raspier. He freed his hand from my grip, caught my chin with his fingers and turned my face back to him. "Hey, I like that you're wet for me."

He pulled my knee toward him, opening my thighs. His hand moved to the crotch of my panties that felt as if they were soaked. I was almost crazy for his touch, but I tensed and squeezed my eyes shut, dreading it as much as I wanted it.

"It's normal," he repeated. "Relax now." He pushed the silky fabric aside and his hand cupped my sex. "Oh, baby, you really are so wet...."

He rested the heel of his hand on my pubis and carefully parted my labia with his fingers. My breathing grew shallow. I lay perfectly still. A finger eased into me. My hips lifted reflexively toward his hand even as a little squeak burst out of my throat.

"Mmm. Tight. Oh, that's good, baby. And your pussy's swelled and hot. I do like that."

I had never heard such words from a man's mouth. I wanted to gasp and blush, but a steady pulse had begun to drum deep in the top of my sex beneath his hand and that nebulous place low in my belly was already faintly convulsing. *Oh, God*. This was getting so out of control.

His finger withdrew from inside me and swept my vulva with long, languid strokes, wetting me even more. I hadn't been touched this way in *sooo* long. Or truthfully, I hadn't been touched in quite *this* way at all, ever. No guy with whom I'd had sex had ever fondled me so tenderly or so expertly. I gave a weak moan.

Then, those agile fingers moved to my clitoris and began gently circling. My focus narrowed and suddenly I didn't care if that speeding train Drake had mentioned crashed right through those thick plate-glass windows as long as Tack didn't stop. I was ready to beg him for something, anything. I could come like this. Any minute. I gripped his biceps and arched my back.

"Am I doing it right?" he asked softly.

I didn't know if he was doing it "*right*," but it felt flawlessly wonderful. "Yesss." The word came out of my mouth a hiss.

"Watching you come is all I've been thinking about all-day."

No, no, no. Too private, too personal. I summoned my voice in a breathy reply. "No, you haven't. You've been looking at a horse."

"Uh-huh. And that just made it worse. After teasing the poor bastard into such a frenzy that he nearly tore up the barn, they didn't even give him a live mare. They led him to a phantom horse and a phony vagina. The whole time he was snorting and pumping and raising hell, I wished that phantom mare was you and I was him."

Something had to be wrong with what he had just said, but with his hand pressuring my pubis and with what his fingers were doing, I couldn't muddle through it. I shook my head. "We can't do this. I'm serious. Look at this sofa. No telling what it cost."

"We'll stop before it gets messy."

It was already messy. I was soaking wet.

All at once, his fingers left me with my clitoris throbbing and my vagina clenching. I barely kept myself from pleading for him to finish what he started. He lifted his fingers to his mouth and sucked on them.

I had never seen anything so primitive. I stared, then shook my head vehemently, releasing the little noise that had stuck in my throat.

"Do you know how good you taste?" He rubbed his wet fingers over my lower lip. I frowned and jerked my head to the side. "Lick your lips, baby. See how good you taste."

Tentatively, I tested with the tip of my tongue and found a salty-sweet taste, not altogether unpleasant.

"See?" he said.

I only looked back at him, saying nothing. He kissed me again and dipped his tongue into my mouth, sharing more of my own juices.

You've just crossed another line, my inner voice warned me.

His fingers tapped my hip. "Lift up a little." I lifted my bottom, allowing him to push my skirt and my half-slip all the way to my waist, exposing my belly above the edge of my bikini panties.

He gave the inside of my thigh a gentle squeeze and smiled down at me. "That's better. Open your legs a little more..."

As if I had become a person with whom I wasn't acquainted, I let my outside knee fall to the side, shamelessly exposing my hot, swollen sex. At this moment, opening my thighs to a total stranger felt like the thing to do. I was beyond doing otherwise.

He pulled my leg over his thigh. His hand came up, slid beneath the waistband of my panties and cupped my sex, again pressing and circling my pubis with the heel of his hand. That odd feeling deep inside my sex returned and clawed at me again. *Oh, yes.* I could definitely come like this.

But a semblance of sanity made another heroic effort and broke through the erotic haze I had fallen into. I would die if Paul appeared and, God forbid, caught us. "Listen, Paul could come up and—"

"He's not coming up here," he whispered, his mouth against my ear. "Be still now...." His finger began to rim my opening. "This is where I want to put my tongue. Think about it...."

Tongue? A shiver shimmied all the way through me. I completely forgot about Paul.

The finger slid into me, followed by another, stretching me and working inside me. "Ooh..."

*Then, In....And in....And in....And over and over....*Liquid heat surged through my veins and I whined and wished for his fingers to be the big, thick cock I had imagined him to have. I was on the brink again, mindless and helpless. The renewed tension that had coiled in my belly had almost become a cramp. I braced my outside foot on the floor, levering my knee to open myself wider. "Oh.... Oooh.... Tack....please..."

"Pull your other knee back a little more....."

Dignity and modesty had forsaken me. The throbbing core of my sex had taken control of my body and brain. I obeyed his orders and hooked my ankle over the back of the sofa.

The pad of his thumb found the demanding bud at the top of my sex. "Is this what you want?"

"Yes," I whimpered.

He applied just the right pressure. "Tack! Oh, Tack!"

"Go ahead, baby....Just let go...."

I did and orgasm billowed through me in great waves, making my hips undulate and my vagina clench against his fingers. My head fell back. I grunted breathless little mews until it ended.

I was a mess, a trembling, embarrassed mess. How many women did he know who climaxed almost instantly with nothing more than the touch of his fingers?

"Good, baby. That felt good to me, too."

And while I was still spinning in a post-orgasmic daze, his warm lips began moving over my neck and jaw. "You were trying so hard. You wanted it bad. How long has it been for you?"

"What?...I don't know..."

"A while, I could tell."

Oh, hell. I hated that.

"Just be still now. You've got lost time to make up. I want you to come again."

"I—I can't..."

"Yes, you can. I'll show you. Just be still...."

With his free arm, he caught my neck in the crook of his elbow immobilizing me and his fingers found that super-sensitive spot that only BOB had found. I gasped loudly and my hips involuntarily lifted toward his hand.

"Ah, that's it, right" he said softly.

I couldn't have answered if I wanted to. Every rational thought had fled from my brain.

He nipped at my earlobe, still stroking inside me. "Just be still, now..."

His thumb began to rub my clitoris again. A guttural noise escaped my throat. I dug my fingers into his shoulder, trying to hold myself in check when everything below my navel had become one greedy vessel of sensation. From a great distance, the fact that Mr. Tack Tackett was not unknowledgeable of female anatomy came to me.

Did I really want to give myself to a man so practiced at seduction and sex?...And on an extremely expensive sofa that didn't belong to me?

No, I answered and stiffened. "Tack, that's enough. Don't—"

"Shh. Just a minute..."

He claimed my mouth again with a sexual rhythm, leaving not even a tiny part of it unexplored, never relenting with agile fingers, rubbing me inside and out. That need deep in my belly already had me in its grip again and I was climbing and climbing. My tiny desperate core felt as if it had grown to the size of a golf ball. My body was quaking. My heart was pounding. Something out of control and scary was going on inside me. I wrenched my mouth away from his. "Tack!..." I grabbed his shirt front for an anchor. "I'm— I'm...coming apart..."

"I've got you, baby," he crooned, his deep husky voice a sonnet. "You're okay...Let it happen...."

I couldn't have stopped it if I had wanted to. Orgasm boiled up like magma and exploded through my body. My vagina clenched violently against his finger. My hips bucked in an uncoordinated rhythm. I panted, unable to control my breathing. Muscles deep inside me began convulsing without let-up and I thought I would go mad. *Oh, God. It hadn't been like this with BOB.*

"Stop!" I sobbed out.

Instantly, he withdrew his fingers, leaving me with an excruciating emptiness. His hand clutched my nape, bringing the strong scent of sex to my nostrils as he pulled my face against his neck, whispering soothing, if dirty, words. "You're so good....Your clit is so sensitive....Aw, baby, you're so easy."

Easy? That was the only word that stuck. I hadn't heard anyone say I was so easy, especially not at the times I hadn't been able to climax at all. I wanted to ask what he meant by that, but I was hardly up to a clinical discussion. I was shaken. I had never climaxed so hard. And I was mortified by my wanton reaction to nothing more than his fingers.

He tipped my chin up and placed a tender kiss at the corner of my mouth. "I knew you'd blow my mind when you finally let go," he said hoarsely. "From here, it only gets better. I promise."

As I calmed, reality started to sneak back into my mind. How long had it been since we left the lobby? "I'm serious," I said, my voice tiny and weak. "We have to get back downstairs."

He heaved a sigh, sat up, pulled a handkerchief from his back pocket—I couldn't remember the last time I had seen a man with a handkerchief—pushed my thighs apart, wiped between them, then wiped his hands. On the handkerchief, I spotted a monogram: *HOT*. Under different circumstances, I would have thought that uproariously funny.

He placed a chaste kiss on my lips, then smiled down at me. "I thought that was good. What'd *you* think?"

I could be your slave for life.

I closed my eyes and arched my brow. I could barely breathe, much less discuss what he had just done to me. I was amazed he had found BOB's secret spot....And his fingers had felt so much better than the gel dildo.

"Not talking?" he asked.

I wanted to say, *no human being has ever made me come like that*, but all I could do was stammer. "It—it was....No one's ever...I've never—"

He leaned in and tenderly kissed me. "I understand. It's gonna be even better when we get to a bed and fuck. I promise."

He told me to lift my bottom again. I did and he straightened my wet panties. He tugged my slip and my skirt into place, then reached down for my shoes. He slipped them onto my feet, stood and pulled me up from the sofa. Still hanging onto to me, he bent and wiped the cushion with his handkerchief.

"Is it wet?" I asked anxiously.

He grinned and gave my lips a quick smack. "You worry too much."

I didn't want to know if we had marred the sofa. I had the dumb idea that not knowing would give me plausible deniability. I stepped away from him and found my balance on my high heels. God, I could fall apart any minute. Though my knees had all the security of Jell-O, I shifted my hips to help my skirt smooth down. Lap wrinkles still creased it even after I tried to iron them out with my flattened hands. My blouse was askew. He pulled the silk panels together and began to button it.

"I can't even imagine how my hair looks," I mumbled, reaching behind myself to unzip my skirt and tuck in my blouse tail. I stole a glance at his bulging fly.

He saw me looking and smiled. "Don't worry about it. It'll keep a little longer. You okay now?"

I had plenty not to be okay about, but straightening my collar, I swallowed hard and nodded.

My unleashed hair fell around my shoulders. He picked up a small sheaf of it and fingered it. "I do love your hair. It feels like silk."

My barrette and the Skyline key ring lay on the sofa cushion. I reached down for the barrette, pulled my hair back into a messy ponytail and clipped it. "There's no hope for it," I said as I reached down for the keys.

"It's great. It looks healthy and sexy." Smiling, he leaned down and kissed me sweetly. "Let's go."

I turned off the lights, we stepped into the hallway and I closed the front door behind us. His hand reached for mine, but I brushed it away. "You can't touch me in the hallway. Cameras, remember?"

"My hotel room doesn't have cameras. I'll bet you haven't eaten all-day. I'll have supper sent up."

Supper. The evening meal. I grew up hearing the word, but I knew very few people in the Metroplex who ever said it these days. The fact that he did touched a tender place within me and reminded me that he and I had that common bond that West Texans seemed to have.

"Your hotel room?" I said stupidly.

"Baby, my cock's aching to get inside you. I can't wait to fuck you to another screaming orgasm. The easiest and quickest way for that to happen is to get to my hotel room ASAP."

He said that as if he were discussing the weather. Was that talk supposed to be foreplay? If so, at the moment, it sounded good to me. Whatever was to happen next with the delicious Tack Tackett was a powerful magnet I didn't have the will to resist.

"That almost sounds like a warning," I said, deadpan.

He gave me a smile that made my weak knees weaker. "It's a promise."

"And I don't recall screaming," I added, ducking my chin as a small grin flitted across my lips.

"Figure of speech. It was music to my ears." He chuckled and kissed my temple.

"Stop," I said, tilting my head away from him. "Cameras, remember?"

We made it to the elevator without further touching each other and stood waiting for the car. "Is there a camera in that elevator?" he asked.

"I don't know, but I wouldn't be surprised. This is a high security building. That's part of the appeal of living here."

The car arrived and we stepped inside. "God, I hope there's no camera. I must look like a wild woman."

"I like the way you look." He tapped his temple. "Up here, I've got an image of you running naked through a forest."

I frowned and gave a little gasp.

"Stop worrying. That concierge is half-unconscious." He grinned mischievously. "He'll never know I just found your sweet spot and finger-fucked you to multiple orgasms.

Sweet spot? Finger-fucked? Good grief! The things he said.

And how many other women has he done that to?

I couldn't help but wonder. He was a breathtakingly beautiful devil who knew way too much about sex.

"And if he figures it out, all he'll do is envy me," he added with a wink.

"Shut-up," I said, unable to hold back a grin. Drake Lockhart might faint if he knew what his good friend and I had just done in his twelve-million-dollar condo, on a sofa that cost God-only-knew how much. My strength—and my cynical sense of the bizarre—was gradually returning.

Tack clasped my hand and interlocked our fingers.

"Cameras," I said and tried to remove my hand from his, but he held it in a tight grip.

We rode to the bottom floor with no more conversation. Having my world rocked had left me with little to say.

As the elevator doors glided open, he let me take back my hand. I looked around for Paul, but didn't see him anywhere. I adjusted my clothing again and tried to neaten my hair. Then I strode toward my table with bravado. He followed.

I gathered the tablecloth off the table and with unsteady hands, haphazardly folded it and struggled to stuff it back into the plastic bag it came in. The thing escaped me as if it had a plan of its own and ended in a heap on the table. I drew a shaky breath and dropped my forehead against my fingers.

He took the tablecloth and the plastic bag from me. In no time, with deft hands and fingers—and if anyone knew just how deft they were, I now did—he had the tablecloth neatly re-folded. He slid it into the plastic bag, zipped it and placed it on top of the box.

I looked up at him for a few beats. There was just something about a guy with a hard-on, who, minutes after what we had just done, could stuff a slick piece of cloth into a slick sack and make it turn out a neat square. Tack Tackett appeared to have self-possession and masculine dexterity in spades. I didn't doubt he could build a house out of toothpicks with one hand and take a woman to an earth-shattering orgasm with the other. And continue to be flaming hot and gorgeous while doing it.

"Thank you," I said. "I guess that does it."

"Where does this stuff go?"

Drake's brokers and I would need it tomorrow. The only place I could think to stash it was in the closet in the concierge's office. But the last thing I wanted was a face-to-face meeting with the building's keeper. "In the concierge's office. But I don't want—"

"I'll take it."

Was he a mind reader on top of everything else? He caught my chin between his thumb and finger, leaned down and smacked my lips. "You're a worrywart. What am I gonna to do with you?"

My inner voice that I had ignored all through the episode on the sofa suddenly piped up. *More of the same?*

Carrying the box, he walked toward the door labeled CONCIERGE at the front of the lobby, giving me a view of his fine butt in his tight jeans. In my mind, I pictured it sans those jeans and shorts. At this point, how could I not?

Boxers or briefs? that ornery inner voice put in.

I closed my eyes, arched my brow and let a great breath escape, trying to reconcile how showing him around Skyline had morphed into going to his hotel and having real sex with him. I hadn't officially said yes, but like a dumb country mouse, I shrugged into my blazer and waited for his return.

Chapter 6

TACK SOON CAME back to the table, clasped my elbow and steered me to the elevator. I let myself be steered. A part of me had always loved the idea of being owned and protected by a strong man willing and able to take control of events and save me from disaster. A puzzling notion because another part of me wondered if I could live with so much *machismo* day-to-day. I had been my own boss for as far back as I could remember. Except for my grandmother and a few teachers over the years, no one had ever told me I should or shouldn't do something.

"Did Paul question you?" I asked.

"He was on the phone. He had no idea what you were doing. My guess is he didn't know you're still here. He's irresponsible. Drake needs to replace him."

Uh-oh. The remarks Tack had made upstairs came back to me: ...*Does Drake know you come up here alone?...If you worked for me, I wouldn't expect you to take chances like this*...

With Tack being good friends with Drake, I had no doubt they would have that conversation. Inside, I winced, uncomfortable with my role in what might happen to Paul. Live-and-let-live was my attitude about the people with whom I worked.

The elevator door opened into the underground parking garage and we stepped out. Only three vehicles occupied the huge empty space—my Ford SUV, a Honda sedan that I presumed belonged to Paul and a white sedan that was obviously a rental car.

While I'd had no trouble allowing Tack unrestrained access to my most private place upstairs, I suddenly had an aversion to getting into the car with him. "I—I'll follow you in my car—" His head shook, but before he could argue, I added, "Then you won't have to bring me back here."

"Is somebody waiting for you somewhere?"

Only Miss Kitty. I had been feeding a feral cat most evenings. She would be hungry and waiting for me to come home. "Well, uh..."

He looked at me expectantly. He probably wouldn't accept a hungry cat as a reason. I frowned. "Why do you ask?"

He shrugged. "I'll deliver you back here tomorrow morning."

Oh, hell! I might be ready, even eager, for a roll in the hay with the delightful Tack Tackett, but I wasn't sure I was ready for the intimacies of a sleepover. "I can't stay the night. And I can't leave my car in this parking garage. It might get towed."

He hesitated, his dark eyes assessing me. No doubt he was trying to figure out if I would really follow him. "Look. What you said upstairs," I told him. "We're both grown people who know what we want. I've already agreed to...it isn't necessary that I spend the night to—to...well, you know what I mean, okay?"

I couldn't bring myself to bluntly say it's just sex and as soon as we do it, I need to go home. He hesitated a few seconds. I doubted he had conceded the debate, but he said, "Which one of these rigs is yours?"

"The SUV."

He placed a hand on my nape as if he feared I might escape and we walked to my SUV. At the driver's side door, I dug in my purse for my keys. He took them from me, opened my door and held it as I scooted behind the wheel. He handed me the keys and closed the door, then leaned down, his hands braced on the roof. "I'll follow you. I'm at the Hilton. You know where it is?"

Mental eye roll. I had lived in Fort Worth ten years and knew the city well. I drove all over everywhere alone and unescorted, but I smiled and nodded.

He poked his head through the window and tenderly kissed me. "Stop worrying. Everything's okay."

"I know."

"Be careful driving." He kissed me again, then stood back and watched me back out.

I drove up the ramp to the exit and sat waiting for the electronic gate to open. That inner voice couldn't resist taking advantage of the silence. *This is bad. As bad as a college hookup, which you said you would never do again.*

The short trip across the city gave the time for me to compose myself. It also gave that protective inner voice more time to lecture me....*Are you cheap or what?....You're doing this for a meal?*

"I haven't eaten since this morning," I mumbled under my breath, watching Tack Tackett's rental car headlights in my rearview mirror.

You can't afford to buy your own supper? This can't go anywhere. Why don't you just go home? You have to get up early tomorrow, dress and come back to the open house by noon. You're causing yourself unnecessary inconvenience. And there's no one to feed Miss Kitty.

I refused to listen. I enjoyed attention from a sexy, good-looking male. Other than a handshake, I hadn't felt a man's touch in more months than I could count and I had been in a state of lust for it all-day. For some reason, my body had chosen *this* man over others, even if it was only for a one-night-stand.

Maybe my subconscious was at work. Maybe deep down, a "hookup" was all I wanted. Like him, I didn't have the time for anything more and I didn't want the hassle of having a demanding man in my life. Been there, done that.

Besides, my car was on autopilot. It didn't want to change directions.

Fifteen minutes later, I parked in a slot in the Hilton's parking lot. He came to my door, offered his hand and assisted me out of the car. "I look terrible," I said. "I hope no one I know sees me."

He placed his hand on the small of my back and urged me along. "You look like you just had a helluva good time. But that's only for me to know and others to wonder about."

I gave him a pointed look over my shoulder. "Seriously?"

We reached the entrance to the hotel and started across the lobby toward the elevators. The lower two floors were familiar. I had been here a few times for various parties and events. Formerly the Hotel Texas, the old building had been remodeled and updated by Hilton, but it still had an historic air about it. People who had been around downtown Fort Worth years back had told me that much of its original appearance remained.

With it being the dinner hour, the lobby teemed with milling people. I was certain every visible person on the lower floor stared at us and knew what we were up to. My heart drummed a steady tattoo inside my ears. I prattled aimlessly, trying to show nonchalance I didn't feel. "Did you know this hotel is where JFK spent his last night on earth? He and Jackie slept in an executive suite the night before they flew to his doom in Dallas."

"I did know that, but that's not why I picked it. There's a Ruth's Chris steakhouse here and I'm in the mood for a good steak. You like steak, don't you?"

And what if I didn't?

I was starting to realize one thing about Tack Tackett. He didn't debate or discuss. Whether the reason was because he had a touch of OCD or something darker, I hadn't yet figured out.

"I'm a total carnivore," I answered.

"Good. I like a woman who's willing to kill to eat."

I glowered up at him. "What?"

He squeezed my side and gave me a wink. "I'm kidding, baby, I'm kidding. My corny jokes are supposed to make you chill out a little."

As the elevator door glided shut, he pressed the button for the twelfth floor and the car lifted off. He took my hand and interlocked our fingers. Only the two of us being in the elevator was a good thing. So much anticipation and sexual tension charged the air around us, sparks could start flying any minute. With great effort, I settled my mind on the fact that I had never been above this hotel's lower two floors.

"You're too quiet," he said.

I might have suddenly lost my voice, but my nerves were jangling like a dinner bell. The closer we got to our destination, the worse the anxiety got. My good-girl persona didn't want to face why I was here. I wished I could blame it on alcohol, but I hadn't had a drop. "I, uh...I'm fine."

"Look at me," he said and I looked up into his eyes. "You can still chicken out."

No! I want this. He had given me a taste of how sex could be and I was hooked. I inhaled deeply and willed myself to try to relax. "I don't want to."

"Thank God." One side of his mouth turned up in that smirky grin. "Because baby, if you walked off, I think I'd break down and cry."

Then, four doors up the hall from the bank of elevators, we were at the door to his room. He unlocked it with his key card and stood back for me to enter a richly decorated sanctum that looked huge even though furnished with two king-size beds. He no sooner shut the door before I kicked off my shoes and we went at each other, mouths plundering, breaths soughing, his arms holding my body tightly against his, his hands kneading my bottom.

We parted long enough for my blazer and blouse to disappear. "I should let you know I've never been very lucky at sex," I said breathily, as I fumbled to unhook the last of his shirt buttons.

He whipped off his shirt and tossed it onto a chair. "What's luck got to do with it?"

His arms slid around my hips and he gripped my bottom, lifted me off the floor and lugged me to the edge of the nearest king-size bed. Reaching down with one hand, he threw back a thick duvet and deposited me on the sheets. He clicked on the lamp, shedding amber light across the room.

I quickly sat up, my greedy gaze locked on his honed biceps and sculpted chest, tanned and glowing golden in the room's low light. My elevator assessment hadn't been wrong. His body was even more beautiful than I had imagined.

His smoldering eyes burned into mine. He bent over, hopping on one foot, then the other, prying off his boots and stripping his socks, his arm and chest muscles rippling with his movements.

He straightened, removed his watch and laid it on the bedside table. Then he pulled a black wallet from his back pocket, dug out foil packages—I couldn't see how many—and dropped them and the wallet on the table. Thank God he had condoms because I had none. Some of my girlfriends carried them in their purses, but I did not. Why would I? Unplanned sex—or for that matter, sex of any kind—wasn't routine for me.

With no hesitation, he unbuckled his belt, shucked his jeans and tossed them to the side. A gray knit tent hugged his manly shape in the front of his boxer briefs.

My mouth went dry and I swallowed hard. *That will not fit*, my inner voice told me.

He sank to the edge of the mattress opposite me. The knit tent stood like a column between us. Surely his erection couldn't be as enormous as it appeared.

"You're wearing too many clothes." He reached out and tugged my cami's spaghetti straps down, but couldn't drag the skin-tight Spandex past my breasts. For a few seconds, he stared at the lacy garment. "Jesus, this thing's worse than a suit of armor."

"Just a minute." I quickly pulled the straps back up on my shoulders, crossed my arms, grabbed the hem and pulled the obstructive garment over my head, baring my upper body. My breasts were larger than most women's of my stature and I was happy to say, they didn't sag. They trilled at being freed after being bound all day and my nipples instantly peaked.

Before I could lower my arms, he made a guttural sound, grasped my elbows and shoved them above my head against the headboard. "Christ, Miranda, I've never wanted a woman as much as I want you."

Before I could say a word, he leaned into me, claimed my mouth and filled it with his tongue. I was still hanging onto the camisole. It slid from my fingers and I neither knew nor cared where it landed.

His tongue explored every part of my mouth. When we parted for breath, he still held both of my wrists in a vise-like, one-handed grip against the headboard. With the other, he cupped one breast in his palm and gently lifted it, brushed my firm nipple with his thumb. "I knew your breasts would be beautiful." He looked up into my eyes. "But you shouldn't wear that thing. It's too tight. It's left imprints on your skin." His fingers lightly moved over my breast. "Doesn't it hurt?"

For the second time he had remarked about my comfort, but I had no interest in how tightly that cami fit. "I don't notice," I murmured, lost in the feel of his fingers on my skin and the distant quickening that had started between my thighs.

He pressed his nose against my underarm and inhaled deeply. Then he licked me. *Licked* me! Little prickles pinged through my body and a silent *O* formed on my lips.

His mouth moved over and he drew the flesh of my breast into wet, wonderful warmth and I shivered. He tenderly licked, gently sucked. The deep tingle inside my sex had become a drumbeat. I wanted badly to touch him, to comb my fingers through his soft hair. I flexed my captured hands. "Let me go...."

"Not yet." He pulled back and watched himself roll my nipple between his thumb and fingers, plucking and molding until the rosy nub was outrageously extended. "Amazing," he mumbled. "Will this make you come?"

After multiple stupefying orgasms on the sofa back at Skyline, if he had asked me if I was ready for another, I might have said no, but with his hand owning and caressing every part of my breasts in places I hadn't even known were so sensitive and sending current straight to my core, another climax was all I could think of. And I was growing edgier by the minute. "I don't know," I breathed.

"Let's see..."

He ducked his head, took my nipple into his mouth again and tongued it madly. His fingers tugged my opposite nipple, then firmly squeezed. At the same time, he pressed the sensitive nub firmly against the roof of his mouth and sucked it hard, only just bordering on causing pain. A sweet pleasure-pain zinged straight to my clitoris and a mini-orgasm hit me unexpectedly. My sex clenched against a profound hollowness and I let out a little cry. I squirmed and flexed my hands. "Please," I panted. "Let me go..."

He released my wrists and my nipple with an imagined small pop, licked into my mouth and enveloped me in an embrace, pressing my bare breasts against the hard wall of his furry chest. I clung to him, waiting for the trembling inside me to wane.

"I didn't—I didn't think I—I could do that again," I stammered. "That was crazy."

He chuckled softly, his breath brushing my temple. "A dozen times, remember?"

He held me close, his nose buried against my neck, one arm tightly around me, the other clasping my nape while he cooed sexy, calming words. He soon sat back and straightened, looking at my chest with a solemn expression. He had made both nipples red and wet, stretched and incredibly firm. "Beautiful," he said, as if he were proud of his handiwork. "But you're still wearing too many clothes."

With a strong arm around me, he pushed me down against the pillows and stretched out alongside me. His hand moved around and behind me, finding my skirt button and zipper and undoing them. He rolled me and lifted me and soon had my skirt and my half-slip off, leaving me wearing nothing but my black bikini panties and my gray stockings. "Sexy," he mumbled. "This is what I wanted back at Skyline."

His fingers eased under the damp elastic top of my stocking. He carefully peeled it down and off, then moved to the other one. As his fingers trailed back up my leg, his tongue flicked a path down my middle. In seconds, he had caught the elastic waistband of my panties with his fingers and just like that, I was naked and at his mercy. A new surge of adrenaline bombarded my system.

He crawled over me, kneeing my legs apart. Instinctively, I accommodated him. His elbows flanked my shoulders supporting his weight. The knit fabric of his shorts that covered his erection didn't hide how hard and hot it felt against my naked sex. I slid my arms around his middle and my legs around his hips, bringing his hard penis even closer to where I wanted it. "I feel so empty," I whimpered.

"I know," he said softly. "I've got a remedy for that."

His hands clasped my head, holding it still as he continued to kiss me. His lips molded my mouth to his, his teeth nipped, his tongue dueled with mine. He was an incredible kisser. I moaned into his mouth, grinding my sex against him. His mouth soon tore away and trailed down, nuzzled my breasts. My nipples were still swollen and tender and I made a small sound.

"Did I make you sore?"

I had no intention of complaining. "I'm okay."

He moved his mouth on down my middle, kissing and licking. "Mmm, your skin's so soft....It smells like flowers..."

Thank the Lord for lavender body wash.

The tip of his tongue dipped into my navel. On a hum, I lifted my stomach to him and he took full advantage, biting and licking and sucking bites of me into his mouth. I vaguely pictured my pale stomach covered with purple hickeys, but so what? No one would see them and what he was doing felt too good to bring it to a halt.

He scooted on down, his lips moving over my belly. "I'm going to tongue-fuck you," he whispered....

This is where I want to put my tongue. Think about it....

Oh, my God. He meant that.

Desire swept through me. Even so, I was a little scared. No man had ever done that to me or for me. Sex with the only lover with whom I had ever had a real relationship had hardly been raw and dirty. Donald had been repulsed by the very idea of his face between my thighs. Though I had been on the pill during the time we were together, he had used condoms because they made intercourse less messy.

Before I could make a decision whether to let Tack go on, he eased my knee up. All at once, I thought of how I must smell after being hot and wet most of the day. I tried to move my knee and shift away from him. "Wait, Tack. Don't...no...you shouldn't—"

His hand tightened on my knee. "Why not?"

I was totally vulnerable. And I was beside myself. I shook my head. "You don't know me....It—it was early this morning when I showered and—"

"I'm not worried about that....I do know you..." He pushed my knee to the side and my sex opened.

"It's more than that....I haven't...no one's ever..."

"Just don't stop me..."

With a sigh, I closed my eyes and surrendered. I wanted this. And even if I didn't, at this point, did I have a choice?

He took his slow and easy time with lush, open-mouthed kisses and nips with his teeth and little sucks along my inner thigh. I rewarded him with huge sighs and tiny moans. After he had thoroughly kissed one thigh, he moved to the other.

Then I felt his fingers stroking my labia. I came up on my elbows to see my thighs wide open and him watching his fingers. Seeing and feeling sent a new surge of adrenaline through me, but my cheeks flamed. "Tack, this is embarrassing me....God....You shouldn't..."

His fingers stilled. He looked up at me, his eyes ablaze. "You're beautiful here, too, you know...." His head lowered and his mouth moved over my vulva, his heavy breath gusting warm against my wetness. "A dozen times. Remember?"

My own breath was coming fast and shallow. "But I don't expect—I didn't think...you meant it."

"A promise like that...I mean it...."

Before I could raise another point, he licked into my sex. Like an electrical shock, sensation zinged all the way to my toes. A delicious and unrelenting clenching set off inside my vagina. I gasped and fell back against the pillows.

He draped my knees over his shoulders, slid his hands under my bottom and lifted me to his mouth.

He sucked my fevered labia, one side, and then the other. His wicked tongue parted my sensitized deeper layers and licked each one. Oh, he was an expert with his mouth at far more than kissing. All the while he ate at me, he groaned softly. That maddening build-up was going on low in my belly. I writhed. My hips undulated shamelessly. Sounds I didn't recognize crawled out of my throat.

"Hold still," he mumbled against my sex.

"I can't. You're driving me crazy."

Then he touched one side of my clitoris with his tongue. My sex clenched, my breath caught. "Oh!" I cried.

The greedy little bud strained forward, desperate for his attention. Just an inch or two to the left. That's all it would take. I struggled to sit up, but couldn't. "Tack," I panted. "I need...please....I need..."

"Impatient girl," he mumbled. "Begging me..."

I was lost in a sea of sensation. My blood was simmering in my veins. He found the other side of my clitoris with his tongue, but still left the tiny kernel desperately needing. "Tack, pleeeze..."

Instead of giving me what I begged for, his nose moved down the length of my sex. His tongue found my quivering opening and slid inside me.

A spume of new pure pleasure as I had never known it coursed through me and I moaned. My hungry vaginal muscles clutched at the invading organ, trying to draw it deeper. He suckled and licked, his tongue speared in and out, the shallow penetration not nearly enough to please the needy slut I had become. I keened, I panted. My fingers clawed at the sheets. "Ooh,..Ooh... oooh, no, don't...Oh, God, don't stop..."

Everything below was in chaos. My sex was clenching, my clitoris was throbbing, both frantic for his attention. I thrust my hands between my knees, gripped a double fistful of his soft hair and tried to maneuver his mouth to where I wanted it the most. My pleas became chants. "Tack...Please, Tack...oh, Tack....Tack, do something..."

When his tongue pulled out of me, I keened in protest.

His fingers quickly replaced his tongue and instantly found BOB's spot deep inside me. I gasped out.

His fingers worked in and out and at the same time, his tongue found my clitoris again, lapped and lashed. The flames of desire licked at me. "That's it...oh, yes, that's it....Oh, Tack, please..."

His fingers continued to thrust in and out of me and finally, finally, he drew my swollen core all the way into his mouth. A violent explosion tore from the soles of my feet to the top of my head, shooting me so far into space I might not return. My toes curled. Deep spasms quaked my body. I sobbed. I anchored my fists in his hair and pulled my knees up as far as possible. I tried to hold back the animal sounds that were escaping my throat, but I couldn't. It went on and on. At the peak of it, tears leaked from my eyes and all I could do was whimper his name.

Then it was over. I had climaxed profoundly, but my sex was still clenching against the emptiness. I wanted his hard cock inside me, fucking me into an even more profound oblivion. I wanted him to hold me, to kiss me. I wanted this to be more than what it was. I wanted him to *feel* something. I craved all of this at once. I had nothing to cry about, but I couldn't stop the tears that trailed past my temples. I gave a little sniffle.

"What is it, baby?"

"Please....I feel so empty...I—I need you—"

"Tell me what you want," he said hoarsely.

"You know..."

"Say the words."

"I—I can't..."

"Yes, you can. Say them."

I had never said dirty words during sex, but I choked out, "Fu—fuck me. Please....And hurry..."

He turned to his side, shoved his shorts past his butt and kicked his legs free. He reached across me, his long, swollen penis bobbing and brushing my thigh as he grabbed a condom off the bedside table.

In seconds, he was standing on his knees between my thighs, giving me a front-row view of his erection— thick, deep red and long enough to reach my heart. He closed his fist around the thick shaft and pulled at it. "Is this what you want?"

Every inch of it. I nodded. "Yes, yes. Just hurry."

He ripped the foil package open with his teeth. I watched, fascinated by those agile fingers quickly covering his thick length with latex.

Then, he was leaning over me, braced on one hand beside me and carefully placing his penis at my opening and scalding me with the heat of the smooth head.

A shudder passed over his shoulders. "Jesus," he choked out. "I thought I'd lose it before we got to this point."

A pulse beat rapidly in his neck. My own heart was pounding. Gripping his thick biceps with my hands, I pulled my knees up in invitation and he pushed the wide head into me. He was so big I expected it to hurt a little. It didn't, but I couldn't hold back a huge sigh.

"Don't stop," I breathed. "Just don't stop..."

"No way..."

He intertwined our fingers and pressed them against the mattress on either side of my head. "Open your eyes," he said tightly.

My eyelids jerked open and I met his eyes, black and glittering.

"I want you to see me, to remember who's fucking you."

Until the day I die..."How could I forget?"

He moved high above me and began a steady rock, the root of him pressing my clitoris with each shallow thrust. My world became his wide, golden chest blocking my sight, our comingled labored breaths echoing in my ears, the scent of sex and his maleness filling my nostrils, the thick root of him pressuring and massaging the tiny spot that had become my universe. I caught on to his rhythm, hooked my heels beneath his buttocks and met him thrust for thrust.

"That's it, sweet baby....That's it....Rub that clit against my dick."

I began to climb and in no time, I felt that tickle, that quickening....I was on the edge again.

His grip on my hands tightened. He picked up the pace. I writhed, uncoordinated, and lost the connection. "Arghh!" I cried.

On a growl, he slammed into me all the way to the hilt. I came with a yelp, my hips pumping wildly, my deep vaginal muscles convulsing beyond my control around him.

When it ended, he untangled our fingers and sank to his elbows, his eyes locked on mine. "Jesus. That nearly finished me off....God, baby, your cunt's so fuckin' tight....So sweet."

He felt enormous all the way up inside me, stretching me, filling me top to bottom and side to side. "You feel so big."

"But not *too* big," he said huskily, his dark eyes intense. He began to pump. "Stay with me."

He moved with athletic ease, each push taking the tip of him deeply into me. I entered another dimension. A glorious bliss came over me. My eyes wanted to close, to better savor the indescribable friction going on inside me. But with great effort, I forced them open and held his gaze.

Without missing a stroke, he braced himself on his hands on the mattress beside my shoulders and lifted his torso. His face was flushed, his black eyes glittering. "Put your legs around my waist." Robotically, I did as ordered. "Gonna fuck you hard...."

He drove into me, his lunges powerful enough to lift my buttocks off the mattress and deep enough that his sac brushed against me with each thrust. I hooked my arms around his shoulders and hung on.

That arcane harrying low in my belly began to build again. How could I come again? My body was spent, but the desperation grew and grew until one great starburst erupted inside me. I dug my nails into his shoulders, my heels into his butt and rode the punishing waves of ecstasy.

His release came with a great strain and groan, his body going rigid and still as his penis jerked inside me. From out of nowhere, a visual of semen jetting from the tip of him came to me and for an insane moment, I hated the idea that the receiving receptacle was a latex balloon. A few seconds passed before his arms gave away and his heaving body sank on top of me.

I was exhausted. I was slick with sweat. My bones had liquified. But I hugged him tightly to me, breathing in his distinctive scent. "Oh, my God, Tack," I whispered. "Oh, my God...."

He lay half on, half off me. He, too, was covered with a sheen of perspiration. We lay there in silence for long minutes.

"Jesus, Miranda," he mumbled finally, his voice hoarse.

"I know," I said. From somewhere, a stupid giggle popped out of my mouth. "You shouldn't have set that goal."

"We didn't get there yet," he gasped out. "But the night's still young."

Oh, God. Could I keep up?

He rolled to my side and hauled me with him until we were front to front. His knee thrust between my legs and he caught my thigh and took it across his hip. He pushed my damp hair back from my face with trembling fingers and looked at me with soft eyes. "You're something else."

"I don't know what's come over me. I never was before."

A hint of a smile tipped a corner of his mouth. "I don't know how I held out so long. I must've wanted to be sure it was good for you. Back there at Skyline, I was scared to death you'd say no."

My chest almost wouldn't hold my swelling heart. I strummed his ribs with my fingertips, smiled up into his midnight eyes that now looked calm and serene. "Now I ask you. How many women have ever said no to you?"

"Enough."

"How could that be when you have so much to offer? And you're so persuasive?"

"You think so?"

"I do. You certainly persuaded me."

"I think what I am is stubborn. When I really want something, I have a hard time taking no for an answer. It'd make my day if you said you wanted this as much as I did."

I pressed my fingers into his thick back muscles, lifted my head and gave him a warrior-woman kiss. "I wouldn't be here otherwise."

"You said sex had to have some meaning."

"That's how I feel. I can't help it."

"Fucking me has meaning?"

Everything inside me stilled. What was he asking me? For some reason, I believed that the next words I said were important. I looked soul-deep into his eyes and said, "Of course it does."

Chapter 7

TACK DIDN'T REPLY, which sent a little stab of disappointment through me.

You scarcely know each other, my snarky inner voice snapped. *What did you expect?*

He reached over to the bedside table, picked up his watch and checked the time. "We should order supper before it's too late."

He rolled to his feet and dealt with the condom, then walked to the bathroom, giving me a view of a narrow white butt and wide tanned shoulders. Thick slabs of muscle flanked a deep valley that traveled the length of his spine. I could fall in love with his body even if the rest of him had no appeal.

I flopped to my back, staring at the ceiling. My thoughts whirled so fast I couldn't grasp so much as one thing that seemed real. What *was* that?

It was fucking, my inner voice chided. *Don't make the mistake of confusing it with lovemaking.*

I couldn't count how many times I had come. My body had never been so thoroughly used, titillated and thrilled.

I had planned on getting dressed and going home, but now, maybe not. I wasn't sure I could walk, much less drive my SUV.

When I heard the flush of the toilet, I turned to my side, propped myself on my elbow and rested my head on my hand, waiting for his return. He came out of the bathroom, giving me a full frontal of all that God had given him. *Good grief!*

He took my breath. He truly could be a Greek statue. His tanned torso was toned and padded with defined muscle. Black hair dusted well-developed pecs and whorled down to his groin. He obviously didn't wax or shave his body, which was fine with me. Abs rippled down his stomach. He had those ridges of muscle that traveled from his waist and disappeared into a perfect delta of pubic hair. He was the most perfect specimen of manhood I had ever seen up close and personal. I drank him in.

His penis, still stretched and deep red, nested in a thatch of black, black hair. As incredible as it seemed, I started to think about having it inside me again.

He gave me that familiar half-grin. "Like what you see?"

"What's not to like? You must work out."

He knows he has great body, my snarky inner voice put in. *How many women have seen him like this? And is one of them waiting back in Midland?*

I shoved those questions right out of my mind. No one had twisted my arm and forced me to be here.

He ran his fingers through his hair as if my remark had embarrassed him. "A little. It's a habit left over from the army. I don't go to a gym or anything. I've got some equipment in my house. And I work around the ranch sometimes. Cowboying is a pretty good workout."

Reaching the bedside table, he rummaged in the drawer. His penis was the perfect level for me to reach out and caress him, but I restrained myself.

He came up with a Ruth's Chris menu, sat down on the edge of the mattress and studied it. His wavy hair stuck out in a dozen directions. I couldn't keep from giggling. He looked at me across his shoulder. "What? What's funny?"

I gave him a teasing grin. "Your hair. It's going every which way."

He grinned back at me. He had the cutest grin. His face was so classic and perfect, but when he grinned, it took on a "little boy" look.

"I'll order steaks."

"Great. As long as you don't expect me to go out and kill a cow."

"Another time, maybe."

"Something small is okay with me. I usually don't eat a big meal this late in the evening."

"What, then? A filet?"

"That's fine."

He picked up the wine list, scanned it quickly, then looked at me.

"Whatever *you* like," I said.

He returned to the list. "I'm not an expert on wine. When I eat steak, I usually order burgundy or anything red. There isn't much I don't like."

"Red wine with red meat. Isn't that what they say?"

He smiled, leaned down to me and gave me a sweet kiss. "Is that what they say? Who is this *they* anyway?"

While he ordered dinner and the wine, I picked up the bar menu. Working in a bar and living with my mom's drinking, I had developed a strong caution about alcohol for myself, but I enjoyed making creative cocktails. Of all of the drinks the menu offered, a blueberry mohito appeared to be the most benign. I knew how to make mohitos, had tasted one, but I had never made one with blueberries. I started to imagine how I could make it and serve it at Smoky Joe's.

After he hung up and started to return the menu to the drawer, I handed the bar menu to him.

"Do you want a drink?" he asked.

I shook my head. "The wine will be enough for me. I don't drink much." I scooted to the opposite side of the wide bed. We had made a wreck of it. "I should find all of my clothes before they bring the food."

I got to my feet and reached down for my cami that had somehow gotten to the floor feet away from where I peeled it off. A sweet, deep ache manifested itself between my legs along with a new experience—my clitoris was tender and slightly sore. This night had been full of new experiences and I had the feeling they hadn't ended yet.

I crossed the room to the closet. Sensing his eyes on me made me self-conscious. I dragged a hotel terrycloth robe off a hanger, hid my nakedness and ducked into the bathroom. My reflection in the wide vanity mirror over the sink looked as ugly as I feared it did. My eye makeup was smeared, my pale complexion looked mottled. I doubted I owned enough makeup to cover the whisker burns on my chin and around my mouth. My hair looked as if I had been in a hurricane.

Tack's travel toiletries bag sat open on the end of the counter and I spotted a small hairbrush. I helped myself to it and brushed out the most obvious tangles. If I had my barrette, I could clip the top layers back into a ponytail, but the clip was, no doubt, somewhere in the bed.

I gave up on the hair and tried to wipe the mascara from under my eyes with a washcloth and warm water. Afterward, I looked only slightly better.

I finished washing up and returned to the bedroom. Tack had put on his jeans, but the fly was open and I saw that he was commando. I found that sexy beyond belief. I gave him a teasing grin. "Be careful zipping up. I wouldn't like you wounded."

He looked down at his fly, then back at me and grinned as he zipped up. "I'll keep that in mind."

I walked around the spacious room, picking up my clothing. He came to me and took the garments from my hands, laid them on the foot of the second bed, then untied my robe and slid his hands underneath. I loved his warm hands on my bare skin.

He gently caressed my waist. "I don't want to think you're with somebody, but it's hard for me to believe you're not."

Don't pass up the perfect opening, my inner voice prodded.

"That goes both ways, you know. It's hard for me to believe you don't have a wife and a houseful of kids back in Midland."

"No kids. Just an ex-wife. These days, seems like everybody's got an ex-something."

Of course he had an ex-*something.* No guy as attractive as he was would have escaped a union of some kind. How long were they together? Couldn't have been long. He wasn't that old. I judged him to be over thirty, but under thirty-five. And why didn't he have kids?

"My ex-wife is a long way from Midland," he added. "And I don't have any other exes."

We kissed long and sweetly. When we stopped, I looked into his eyes, cocked my head and asked, "How far is a long way?"

"Germany."

Quick mental exercise. Aggie class ring. ROTC. *Aha. She's in the army.* "Oh. That *is* a long way.

He released me and picked up his shirt from the chair where he had tossed it. He no sooner had pulled it on and buttoned it before the food and the mouthwatering aroma of grilled steak arrived. The steward rolled in a small table on which our meal was laid out, then bustled about, arranging dishes, lifting lids and opening and pouring wine. He moved chairs from the table on the far side of the room. As he started to leave, Tack handed him bills, the denomination of which I couldn't see.

Tack held my chair for me and I sat down. "Hmm. Heavenly. I haven't eaten at Ruth's Chris in a very long time."

He took a seat opposite me, picked up his wine glass and sipped. "Try the wine."

I sipped. "Tastes good to me. I don't have a trained palate, you know."

We settled down to eat. I searched for a place to start a conversation. "What about the condo? Did you and Drake talk about it?"

He picked up a roll that looked to be softer than a pillow. "A little." He smiled. "I've known Drake a long time. I know how he is. We're *dickering*."

So my warning him about Drake's competitiveness wasn't necessary. "Oh, good. Which one are you dicker- ing on?

"The big one on the twentieth floor."

Oh. My. God. A mansion in the sky. Twelve Million dollars. Besides the price, the size variance between the 2,100 square-foot unit on the seventeenth floor and the 6,000 square feet on the twentieth was huge. Why would he need so much room?

I gave him a look. "Seriously? Drake said you wanted a small pad."

"A small pad is all I need for myself. But then I started thinking about the investment and my sister in

Killeen. She's got four kids. Her husband's in Afghanistan. They live frugally. If I had a bigger place, she and the kids could have a good place to stay when stuff is going on here in Fort Worth. Killeen isn't that far away. Or she and her husband could use it as a getaway when he's home. He'd be insulted if I offered them money, but providing a nice place for them to take a break now and then is a small thing I can do for them."

He had buttered the roll he picked up. Arching his brow, he offered it to me.

I frowned, considering. "Hmm. I'll bet the bread here is scrumptious. I usually don't eat bread, especially with butter, but yes, I'll take one."

He smiled, placed the buttered roll on a plate and slid it to me. "Not a drinker, don't eat bread and butter. Why so much discipline?"

"Controlling my weight is important to what I do."

He picked up another roll, pulled it apart and started to butter it. "I thought you were a real estate agent. Now I'm curious. What is it that you do?"

"You *would* ask." I laughed. "I've never been able to describe my business. And even if I try, half the people I tell about it don't believe I could be making a legitimate living."

He looked at me, roll and butter knife suspended, his eyelids narrowed. "Oh, yeah? Try me."

"Well...I'm not a Realtor. I'm an event planner. And a part-time bartender and sometimes model. I help Drake Lockhart out occasionally when he has something special going on."

"Every bit of that calls for more conversation. How does somebody get to be doing all of those jobs at one time?"

"Total accident." I cut into my steak and tasted it. "Yum. This is cooked to perfection."

"You were about to tell me about what you do."

For some reason, I did want him to know a little about me, but only surface information. I sipped my wine. "Okay, I'll give you the short version. When I got out of college, I couldn't afford to sit and do nothing while I sent out resumes and waited for Corporate America to open its arms to me. I had a part-time idiot job with an energy company. I had hoped for an internship or something to develop there, but I must not have known the right people.

"Anyway, one of the big wigs needed to have a cocktail party. He was a widower and without a wife, he didn't know where to begin. He was whining and angsting about it all over the office. So one day when I was helping him find something in the filing cabinet, he said, 'If you'd put this party together for me, Miranda, I'd pay you a couple hundred bucks.'

"I guess he thought that because I was young and just out of college, I knew all about partying. He was joking, but he had no idea how precious that amount of money was to me at that time. So I joked back with him. I said, 'Mr. Burrows, the way things are right now, I'd do almost anything for two hundred dollars.'"

Tack was watching me intently. "So what happened?"

"He said, 'Go for it, little lady. Let me know what you need.' So I did."

Tack smiled and shoved a bite of steak into his mouth.

"Where I come from," I continued, "cocktail parties are something you see in old movies. I watched a couple, got some ideas. In college, research was something I was good at, so I spent the better part of a weekend digging out information online and at the library and on Monday morning, I presented Mr. Burrows with a plan. He liked it, so he arranged for space. I subcontracted with caterers and liquor wholesalers and organized a cocktail party for three hundred people. And to my amazement, it was a huge success. Mr. Burrows got compliments from all directions. And there you have it. A star was born."

I sipped my wine again. "Anyway, after that, I put my name out as a small event planner. That was a few years ago. Now I have a company I call Gala and I'm busier than I ever thought I'd be. I'm starting to move up to bigger and more specialized events. The whole thing is a total accident."

He laughed. Not a belly laugh, but more than a chuckle. "That's great. See? I knew you were more than just a pretty face. And these events are where you tend bar?"

"No, no. If it's something where we serve liquor, I hire someone for that. I work as a bartender myself a few weeknights in a neighborhood cocktail lounge near where I live. It has nothing to do with Gala."

"Why? You said your business is successful."

"The money I make there has a designated place to go. It's money I don't want to take out of my business....So what about you?...No, wait, let me guess. You've got an Aggie class ring, so I'm guessing you were in ROTC. And then you joined the army?"

He smiled. "That's what a lot of West Texas boys do, you know."

"Were you overseas?"

"Two deployments."

He said no more and I chose to leave that topic alone. Many of the vets I knew didn't want to discuss their military service.

"So you live alone in Midland? In a house or an apartment?"

"An old ranch house. Built in the twenties."

"That doesn't surprise me one bit. I see 'cowboy' plastered across your forehead. And if you hang out with Drake Lockhart and his brothers, you're bound to be a cowboy."

"Come on, now. What's wrong with cowboys?"

"Not a thing. I'm just saying you have the look. Do you have cows and everything?"

"A few."

"Do you look after them yourself?"

His head shook. "Don't have time. My dad's there. And we've got a man who lives on the place and helps him take care of things. An older gentleman who's a longtime friend. He pretty much has no family of his own, so he's adopted us. As for my horses, they're usually at the track with my trainer."

"Cutting horses?"

"Racehorses."

Did he say racehorses? Ohmigod. I had never known anyone who owned even one racehorse. "Racehorses? You have real racehorses?"

"Uh-huh. I've got a mare that's been a big winner, but it's time to take her off the track. The Weatherford horse is a good stud with an impressive record. He and my Rosie will give me strong, fast babies."

It dawned on me how close he lived to Ruidoso, New Mexico, where some of the great quarter horse races occurred. "Hah. You want Rosie to give up racing and have babies? Aren't you the chauvinist."

He smiled. "That's what you do with good horses."

Digging for a hint that he might come back to Fort Worth, I said, "You liked that Weatherford horse, then?"

He nodded. "I'm pleased. He's what his owner represented."

He got to his feet and walked over to the bedside table, picked up his wallet and brought it back. He opened it and showed me a snapshot of a shiny red roan that just looked like a champion. I craned my neck to see if he had pictures of women or kids, but I saw none. "She's beautiful."

"Your hair makes me think of her. Pretty. I like that red color."

He liked my hair because the color made him think of his horse? Most of the men I knew liked blue. At times I had wondered if blue was the only color they were able to see. What did it say about him that he liked rusty red?

He looked up at me and showered me with a sweet smile, his pride in the horse bald-faced. "Her name's Dashing Ruby Rose. Her granddaddy is Dash for Cash."

I knew little about horses' names, but I did know that competitive horses often had long names based on breeding history. I tilted my head and smiled. "Ah. That just sounds like she's as fast as she is beautiful. So horse racing is how you make your living?"

He shook his head. "I'd get awful hungry if I depended on my horses. They're a hobby."

And probably every bit as expensive as cutting horses.

"I make my living in the oil business," he added.

"Oh, I see," I said, as if he had revealed something I hadn't already figured out.

"I'm one of those folks the environmentalist movement hates. In the old days, I would've been called a wildcatter, but we've got fancier words now and some science for backup."

Every Texas native, especially a *West* Texas native, knew what a wildcatter was. Gutsy mavericks who drilled for oil on speculation, threw money around like some Arab sheik loose in Las Vegas and thought nothing of making a fortune or losing one all in the course of a day.

I saw a new layer of Tack Tackett. He was a rogue and a gambler. And he would soon be the owner of a twelve-million-dollar condo in Skyline. He was obviously filthy rich. If he had no wife, a guy as sexy and good-looking as he was, and rich to boot, was bound to have a harem following him around.

I didn't want that likelihood to affect my good time. I wanted to hear him talk more about himself. "Does the science eliminate the gamble?"

"Only to a degree. There's always risk when you dig a hole in the ground. I'm a geologist. I think I know what's underneath me, but I can never be sure until I drill."

We had finished our meal and emptied the wine bottle. I was feeling floaty and relaxed. He looked at me intently, "I hope you didn't mean it when you said you couldn't stay the night."

I had meant it when I said it, but now, even if I wanted to do the fifteen-mile freeway drive to my condo, I wasn't so sure I should. The wine had put me in an alcohol buzz. Beyond that, I was enjoying myself immensely. Still, I said, "I have to be at Drake's open house again tomorrow. I really should go."

"Ma'am, you're breaking my heart."

I cocked my head and give him a flirty smile. "Why do I think your heart is too tough to break?"

"You're wrong about that. I'm a cream puff."

He rose, rounded the table and offered me his hand. "I want you to stay. That first go-round took the edge off. I can last longer now."

What could I say to that? So much for my leaving. No good reason to refuse him came to me. Without a word, I took his hand and stood. He led me over to the bed and opened the covers, then slid the robe off my shoulders and let it fall to the floor. Without pause, I crawled between the sheets. He peeled off his shirt and jeans and followed.

He took me into his arms and I lost myself again in his luscious kisses. We rolled over the king-size mattress flesh to flesh, sensuously touching and teasing, with him promising filthy things he intended to do to me and me mewing and cooing my acquiescence. Everything about him excited me—his naughty words, the way he touched with gentle, but knowing hands and fingers, the way he gave and took pleasure.

I could think of nothing I wanted more than to please him. I licked his nipples, savored the salty taste of his warm skin on my tongue. When I sucked them, he groaned softly. I crawled on top of him and edged between his legs.

"What are you doing?"

"Close your eyes."

I assumed he did as I moved my open mouth down, tracing his happy trail with my tongue. I had only heard from Ashley and read on the Internet how to do what I was about to. I let my instincts lead me. His thick, hard cock almost reached his navel. "No wonder I felt so full when you were inside me," I murmured, and brushed my lips over the wide head of him. He was almost hot and felt like velvet against my tongue.

"Mmm..." His hips lifted, giving me his manhood.

I swirled my tongue around him, then fit the tip into his little slit and gingerly sucked the head of him. On a groan, he flexed his hips. "Jesus, Miranda..."

I looked up. He was propped on his elbows watching me, his jaw tightly clenched. Our gazes met. Even as dark as his eyes were, I saw the blatant lust in them.

I had read that the backside of a man's erection was the most sensitive. I licked my way down the backside to the root. His scent filled my nostrils and the crisp black pelt that covered his groin tickled my nose. I closed my hand around the thick shaft and moved my mouth on down to his scrotum.

"Miranda...," he said raggedly. His thighs opened wider and his fingers tangled into my hair.

I took one testicle into my mouth. His erection jerked in my hand. "Miranda," he gasped. "Fuck!...Be careful, baby..."

I wallowed his testicle in my mouth, carefully sucked. His grip on my hair tightened to the point of pain. "Shit," he blurted.

Undeterred, I moved to the other testicle.

His legs and arms shifted restlessly and swear words hissed from his mouth. Finally I licked my way up the back of his shaft again. Closing my hand around the hot velvety thing, I slid my lips over the crest of him. As I sucked, I moved my hand up and down in a steady rhythm.

"*Fuck!*" A rumble rolled out of his chest and his penis thrust forward, filling my mouth all the way to my throat.

My mouth wasn't large enough to take all of him. I clamped down and pulled back to the tip, then slid down again, taking him into my throat and sucking hard. His fingers dug into my shoulder like vises, his hips moved with my rhythm. "Fuck....Aw, God...."

The pressure of his fist in my hair hurt my scalp, but I didn't stop. I loved hearing him grunting and hissing and cussing. The whole process was hot and so was I, my own passion spurred by his.

All at once, his hips jerked up. A growl tore from his throat. "*Jesus God!...Miranda! Stop!* I'm gonna come...."

He gripped my shoulders and quickly pulled himself out of my mouth, his breath huffing, his black eyes boring into mine. "Where did you learn to do that like that?"

"Nowhere. I've never done it before."

His eyes held mine. "You're amazing."

That couldn't have been the best BJ he had ever had. Someone experienced would surely have done it better.

He reached across me and fumbled for a condom on the bedside table and sheathed himself, then quickly crawled over me. "When I come, I want to be inside you."

He slid his arm underneath me and flipped me onto my stomach. Stunned, I yelped into the bed covers.

His arm slid under my belly, lifted me and set me on my knees, thrusting my bottom in the air and gluing my face against the mattress. "Spread your legs some more," he ordered gruffly, kneeing my thighs apart.

I blindly obeyed.

His hands smoothed over my bottom, molding and shaping each half. "God, I love your ass."

His fingers glided down to my sex, stroking and separating as if he were exploring. My already trembly knees weakened and I whimpered his name. Two fingers slipped inside me and began to furiously work in and out, stroking BOB's place, chasing away every rational thought. Then his tongue, unbelievably hard, speared into me in fast stabs. His arms came around my thighs and his fingers found my clitoris. The minute he touched me I was ready again and for a fleeting second, I wondered if I could take him again. Every part of my sex felt swollen and even more sensitized from his earlier attention.

The plush head of him pressed against my opening and he filled me with one hard push. I didn't know he could go any deeper than he had earlier, but I felt him in a place no one had ever been before him. A gruff sound came out of my throat.

He pulled out slowly, teasing me and leaving me empty and desperate. My sex contracted, wanting him. "Don't tease me," I whimpered.

He came back inside me just as slowly as he had left. My vaginal muscles grabbed onto to him and clutched him. Pleasure swept through every part of me.

He began to fuck me in a steady rhythm, slowly at first, but soon his thrusts became faster, harder and deeper, each one brushing BOB's place and pushing me higher on the bed. My clitoris screamed for relief. I began to huff and pant. I tried to raise my upper body, but his hand slid up my spine to the center of my back and held me in place. I had never felt so possessed, so owned. That need and that tightening inside my belly demanded to be sated again.

It went on and on, with me pleading and gasping against the mattress and him rutting into me like an animal.

"Tack, please," I huffed out. "I have to come."

His arm slid around my belly, his fingers found my clitoris. One touch and ecstasy wracked me from head to toe and my sex convulsed wildly. I came with an orgasm that shook me so profoundly I bit down on a mouthful of the bed covers to keep from screaming.

"Fuck!" he barked out and drove deeply into me one more time. His body went rigid for a few beats, then he slumped over me. Seconds later, he eased to my side. "You okay?"

"I think so," I said weakly. I carefully straightened my legs and eased down against the bed, grateful I didn't have to get up and walk. The smell of him, of me, of sex, surrounded me and I kept my face turned away from him as I tried to gather myself.

He grasped my shoulder and turned me back to him, and held me against his chest. I wanted this closeness, needed it. I hugged him tightly until our heartbeats gradually slowed.

"Jesus, Miranda. That knocked my socks off."

All I knew was that if he hadn't owned me before we arrived at the Hilton, he owned me now. I had never felt so gloriously fucked. "And you aren't even wearing socks."

"This is no time to be a smartass." He kissed me again, long and tenderly, his palm holding my face captive, his tongue filling my mouth with slow sensual strokes. When we parted, he looked at me with an intense expression I couldn't read. "You need to rest. Let's get some sleep."

I needed sleep all right. I was spent. He surely was, too. We drifted away, locked in an embrace. "You know something?" I mumbled sleepily. "It's a good thing we're both in good shape.

Chapter 8

My mental clock that never failed me woke me before daylight. I could see almost nothing except the digital clock on the bedside table glowing 5:00 a.m. in red letters. We hadn't called for a steward to remove the table. The comingled smells of sex and grilled steak lingered in the air, making me hungry for two different things.

You've got to be kidding, my inner voice chided. *You won't be able to walk if you fuck him again.*

That much I knew.

I also knew I had to get home. I should have left here before now. My sight began to adjust to the gray light. I eased to a sitting position, placed my feet on the floor and carefully stood. I was sore everywhere. Even my scalp. He'd had a death grip on my hair while I had made love to his beautiful cock.

I gathered my clothing from the end of the other bed and tiptoed into the bathroom. The shower tempted me, but waiting until I got to my own trappings at home would be easier. What I really needed was a bath so I could immerse my overused parts for a long restorative soak.

I stared at Tack's toothbrush, debating if I should use it. Why not? His tongue had been inside my vagina; his penis had been in my mouth. Sharing a toothbrush seemed like a small thing.

Before leaving the bathroom, I paused and considered morning after etiquette. Should I wake him

and say good-bye? It hit me suddenly that I might
never see him again and a burn rushed to my eyes.

*Stop it, stop it, stop it. You knew what this was
from the beginning.*

I banished the would-be tears with a deep sniff. I
needed to leave now. Truthfully, I didn't want to be
distracted by him anyway.

I tiptoed back into the bedroom where I shrugged
into my blazer and stuffed my stockings into my
pocket. I found a hotel notepad and pen. He didn't stir.
I returned to the bathroom and wrote a quick note.

After reading it, I didn't like it. I strained my tired
brain for something witty and sexy and wrote a second
note. I tore it up, too. God, he had fucked me senseless.
"Damn," I whispered. "Get your wits about you,
Miranda."

I shook my head to clear it and wrote a third note:

> *Have to get home and get ready for
> this afternoon's open house. You were
> wonderful last night. Not quite a dozen,
> but the one long one made up for the
> shortfall.*

I ended it with a smiley face.

From my purse, I dug out a business card that had
my cell number and my home office number. If he
called me at either number, if I didn't answer, he
would get my voice mail where he could leave a
message. I laid my note and my card on top of his
toiletries bag.

Then, rather than flush the toilet again, I gathered
the pieces of the torn-up notes and stuffed them into
my blazer pocket, too. Carrying my purse and shoes, I
eased through the doorway and pulled the heavy door
closed behind me. In the hallway, I slipped on my
shoes without stockings and made my way to the
elevators. My feet and ankles were so sore from
yesterday, I was almost limping.

While I had never awakened in a hotel room with
a strange man, at least I wasn't in a totally strange
place. I knew how to get home. On a Sunday morning
at 5:30, freeway traffic was light, giving my mind an

opportunity to sort all that had happened in the past twenty-four hours.

I'd had moments in which I pondered how life could change in the blink of an eye. I had experienced a dozen of those moments the past day. This time yesterday morning, I'd had no idea I would meet a man good-looking beyond description and rich to boot or that he would be so skilled, so in tune with my body and my desires that he would take me to an ecstasy I hadn't known existed.

I also was aware of something about myself that was new. Yesterday, I knew I was naïve about sex. Today, I realized just how naïve. I had chattered with various girlfriends about men and sex uncountable times. Girl talk about men was what single girls did. We, or I should say, *they* joked about BJs, G-spots and a dozen other sex-related topics. One thing stood out in my memory. They talked about how hard it was to find a guy good at mind-blowing sex and how after they had found one, they were reluctant to let him go, even if he was far from perfect or even abusive.

My girlfriends could have talked all day and never imparted what I had learned with Tack overnight. The emotion, the physical feeling—both were indescribable. I felt like a deflowered virgin all over again. I doubted sex would ever be the same with anyone.

Tack's words echoed through my memory....*I love your hair.... I love how you smell.... I love how you taste.... It's better to engage on more than one level....*

Had I been engaged on more than one level? Had he? It had felt as if we both were.

My thoughts did a one-eighty and Donald and his ineptness in bed barged into my mind. I was twenty-five years old the first time I had slept with him and he was five years older. Until then, I'd had sex with exactly four people and no one of them had come close to what I'd read about in books. In the beginning, Donald, or I should say 'we,' had been clumsy. I hadn't known what his previous experience had been. Still didn't. Looking back on it, at thirty years old, it seemed that he should have known more about pleasing a partner than he did.

Over time, he, or we, had become adequate in bed, but on Donald's best days he hadn't compared to Tack Tackett. Part of it, without question, was emotional. Simply put, I had never been in love with Donald. I had stumbled into a physically committed relationship with him, but I had never seen him as my dream man, something I couldn't say about Tack Tackett.

My inner voice berated me. *Dream man? You are so dumb! You cannot let yourself get emotionally invested in a man you'll never see again.*

"But I will see him," I said to the air around me. "I left him my phone number. He'll call."

Phone calls. Crap. Lisa's call of yesterday morning took over my musing. I couldn't rely on her to see that Mom got back on that medication. I stepped back into reality and started to think about the trip I had to make to West Texas.

Mom. I sighed, as I always did when it came to her. My eyes misted. My love for her was more like mother and child than daughter and mother. I couldn't remember a time when she hadn't been a burden, either directly in front of my face or indirectly lurking in the back of my mind. Even when I was a little kid, more often than not, I had been forced to be the adult in the room. To this day, I felt guilty for leaving her and for leaving Lisa.

When I was sixteen, Mom married, Husband #3, Richard Garland, an overbearing brute of a man I had both feared and hated. Richard had moved Mom and Lisa to Abilene, but I stayed in Roundup with my grandmother. At that point, Grandma had started pushing me to save myself.

Mom's marriage to Richard hadn't lasted long. A year later, she and Lisa were back, bringing the chaos that always accompanied my mother.

The year that followed that was a fateful year. My grandmother passed from a sudden heart attack, leaving everything she owned in a trust for my mother's benefit. Her estate hadn't been large—a little bit of cash in the bank, her house, an aging Cadillac and a few acres of farmland leased for cotton growing. I graduated from high school that year and left Roundup the day after graduation. A few months later,

Mom married Darrel Jones, an old high school friend who had become a second-rate lawyer. It had taken him and Mom no time to break my grandmother's trust and take ownership of her assets.

By the time her marriage to Darrel ended, all Mom had left was Grandma's old house and an aged Cadillac.

Indeed, I might have left her and Lisa, but I hadn't escaped. For the ten years I had been gone, I had still dealt by long distance with Mom and her problems—her highs and lows, a new marriage to Husband #4, then said husband divorcing her. As for Husband #5, no one even knew she had married him until after she had already done it.

Would I ever be able to escape? I had asked myself the question a thousand times. Where Mom and indirectly, Lisa, were concerned, I saw no light at the end of the tunnel. At the same time I had those thoughts, I also recognized that I enabled them both, and even Arnie. But I didn't know how to stop. They needed me.

Their needs frequently had come between Donald and me. The mess that was the relationship I tried to have with him finally became as much my fault as his. Had he cheated because he sought relief from the pressure that my family brought to my doorstep? Was someone less encumbered than I was easier for him to be with?

So if the answers to those questions was "yes," he hadn't really loved me and it was just as well that he was out of my life.

Could *any* man have the tolerance to put up with me and my family? Though an answer to the question had never come, I had learned one thing from the experience with Donald. I could never again allow a man I cared about to get involved with my family.

My thoughts veered back to Tack Tackett and a long string of "even ifs." Even if Tack were a guy who *could* care about me...even if Lisa got a job or found a husband...yada, yada, yada. Then there was Mom's illness itself. Bipolar disorder had a genetic component. Even if I didn't suffer from it myself, my kids, if I ever had any, could. How selfish would I be to risk that?

Meaningless sex. One-night stands. Dead-end hookups. Was that all there was out there for me?

Mental groan. All of it was depressing and confusing, a conversation not good for much except passing the time as I drove up the freeway.

When I reached my condo, Miss Kitty was waiting for me by the front door. "Hi, pretty girl," I said to her, gingerly squatting to rub her head. "Have you missed me?"

She gave me a long-suffering meow.

"I know I've been bad, baby. I didn't give you supper last night, did I?"

I loved this scruffy orange and white cat. I loved her so much I had captured her a few months ago, stuffed her into a cat carrier and hauled her to a vet to be spayed and I routinely bought her an expensive collar so she wouldn't become flea infested and suffer from one of those flea-borne illnesses. I even bought her the most expensive cat food that was supposed to be healthier. I wished I could make a pet of her. Sometimes I had been able to coax her into the house. She walked in, sniffed or brushed against everything and explored, then wanted to go back outside.

"It was chilly last night," I said as I unlocked my front door. "Where did you sleep, baby? You see, if you'd come live with me, you'd always have a warm place to sleep."

The cat purred and brushed against my legs. I carried cat food out of the utility room, filled her bowl and gave her fresh water. I tried to persuade her to come in, but with her belly full, she wasn't interested.

Finally, worn out, I made my way to the bedroom where I shed my clothes, placed my phone on the lamp table beside my bed and crawled between the covers. A shower could wait.

Three hours later, I awoke, feeling refreshed. I had slept the sleep of the dead. I grabbed the phone and checked the call log. Miscellaneous missed phone calls and voice messages, but none from Tack. *Crap!* Had he already checked out and left town? Should I call the hotel and ask?

Bad idea, my inner voice told me.

After soaking in the tub and doing my hair, I felt human again. I was starving. I went to the kitchen, but before I set out to cook breakfast, I checked the call log on my phone again. Nothing.

A blue funk took root within me. If Tack was going to call me, he should have already. I had believed I would hear from him, but he would be his way home by now. I didn't even know if he had piloted his own plane or if someone else had flown him, but he was surely gone.

I watched the news on a small TV in my kitchen while I cooked and ate an egg white omelet. Then I dressed in a tailored black skirt and a royal blue satin blouse, pulled one side of my long hair back behind my ear and secured it with a blingy clippie. I added gold hoop earrings and a gold chain around my neck. I wanted to look my best. Maybe he hadn't already left town. Maybe he would stop by the open house today.

I made one concession to comfort over vanity. Today, I opted for more sensible shoes. Another full day of those gorgeous pumps I had worn yesterday could cripple me.

At Skyline, three Realtors from Lockhart Concepts were there and ready to go to work, so it appeared my day would be light. That suited me fine. I might try to sneak away before six o'clock. Standing all day held no appeal and might take more effort than I could muster.

Through the day, in slow moments, I called up Tack's name on Google. His whole name was Harvey Owen Tackett. His initials were HOT, just like the monogram on his handkerchief. That still struck me as funny and I couldn't keep from grinning. He was thirty-four years old. He had founded and owned a development company, Tackett Energy Corporation. He drilled for oil all over the world. *Hm. Well-traveled.* I hadn't been out of Texas more than half a dozen times in my entire life.

I checked my phone a dozen times. A few calls, but none from him.

Mid-afternoon, Drake and his beautiful wife came by. I made a point to ask, "So did you sell Mr. Tackett a condo?"

"Not yet. He's a tough customer." He grinned impishly. "But I know him. I'll hear from him. He was impressed with the penthouse unit."

"Yes, he seemed to be," I said carefully, lest I reveal something I didn't want Drake to know. *Twelve million dollars.* I couldn't believe it. Would I ever know if he actually bought it?

Dusk crept in and finally, I accepted, truly accepted, that Harvey Tackett and I had not engaged on more than one level after all. I would never see him again. Even so, I couldn't label what went on between us as casual sex. And I couldn't forget the dozen times he had told me he loved this or that about me. Not the same as the big three words, but still...I didn't want to believe he was a liar.

The common sense part of me argued with me. *What did you expect? Get over it. What would you do with him if you had him?*

∞

Early Monday morning, even before I opened my eyes and got out of bed, I started thinking about my trip to West Texas. I had no firm time to be anywhere until four-thirty when I had to show up for work at Smoky Joe's. I called Joe and explained I had to leave town.

After a glass of juice and a protein bar, I put food out for Miss Kitty. Then I started the day by dragging out the jar where I kept my tip money and counting it. I had over $800 in cash. Not bad for four weekday shifts. Several of my high-roller type customers had been into Smoky Joe's through the week.

Next, I called the two college students who conducted most of the children's parties Gala took on and made sure they were good to go for Wednesday and Thursday.

Ashley, my hairdresser, was next on my list. It was she who kept my long tresses soft, shiny and flowing. I could not afford to have hair that looked like a thatch. Ashley took only friends and special patrons on Mondays. "Come in at two," she told me. "I'll be the only one here."

Last, on deep breath, I called my sister. "What's the latest on Mom and her pills?"

"Nothing new. I already called the doctor, but I had to leave a message."

"You couldn't get her an appointment?"

"Was I supposed to?"

My patience snapped. "Lisa, forgodsake—"

"What?" she barked back.

"Never mind. Did Arnie come back yet?"

"He tried to. He showed up drunk as a lord and sick. Mom and I didn't have the money to go buy him beer to sober up on." Big sigh from Lisa. "Anyway, Mom kicked him out. Told him not to come back."

My jaw tightened. Though I worked in an environment where alcohol flowed freely, I had no patience with drunks. "I'm coming out there," I said. "I've got to see my hairdresser this afternoon, but I'll leave afterward. I should be there by eight or so."

"Well, by all means, don't miss a trip to the beauty shop."

I made no apologies to anyone for being a high-maintenance woman. The way I looked had gotten me where I was. "My appearance is the face of my business, Lisa. You know that, so just stop with the BS. Tell Mom I'm coming."

I disconnected, squeezed into my Lycra workout clothes and drove to the gym. All the while I worked out on the machines, I thought about Tack scantily clad in a "home gym." And I pictured him astride a horse cowboying.

As I stepped off the elliptical machine, I ran into a friend and trainer who worked with me when he had time. Chad Streicher used to be my hairdresser until he gave up the beauty business to become a body builder and personal trainer. In a way, he really hadn't given up the beauty business. He had just changed his focus.

He challenged me to a session of kickboxing. I was tired, but aggression was the perfect outlet for the mood I was in.

After he trounced me, he said, "What happened to the days when you could kick my ass?"

"I already wore myself out on the elliptical machine."

He laughed. "Excuses, excuses. You could use an energy drink."

He dragged me off to the juice bar and ordered me some kind of super energy concoction. Served in a tall clear glass, it was a vivid green. *Loaded with caffeine and sugar, no doubt.* "What is this?" I asked.

"My specialty. Kale and apple and blueberries with green tea and a large scoop of vanilla protein powder."

I wiped perspiration off my face with a towel and sipped. "Hm. Tastes better than it looks. This is *your* recipe?"

"Sure is. Good, huh? I push it to all of my victims. So, whatcha been doing?"

Hah. If you only knew. I rarely discussed my personal life with anyone except Ashley. "Same old, same old. What's new with you?"

He smiled and gave me a shy look. "Um, met a new friend."

For him, a new friend was a boyfriend. "Really? How did that happen?"

"I got introduced to him at a party Saturday night. We really hit it off. He invited me home with him. It was a one-time-deal, but..." He shrugged and grimaced.

"That wasn't a good idea?" I sipped more. I was feeling better.

He gave a huge sigh. "Is a one-night-stand ever a good idea?"

Ouch. Today, that question hurt.

"I really like him and I think he likes me," Chad went on. "I want him to respect me, but since I went home with him when I'd just met him, I'm afraid he'll think I just fuck everybody."

Crap! I stared into my glass, the green liquid suddenly looking less than fortifying. "That's a common problem, no matter which gender you like."

"Oh, my God, Miranda. Why did you say that? Did you fall off the wagon?"

I had forgotten that Chad was almost psychic and besides that, he knew me well. I shook my head and looked away, swallowing back the burn behind my eyes.

"You're too hard on yourself, Miranda. You need to cut yourself some slack."

"I don't know what I need. But something I don't need is to spend the night with someone if it's going to make me feel like this."

"Stop beating yourself up, babygirl. Everyone needs a human touch now and then."

I nodded. "You can't un-spill milk, right?"

"So who was the lucky dude?"

"Business associate. From out of town, thank God. I'll never see him again. You wouldn't know him."

Chad's brows climbed up his forehead. "Uh-oh. Hope he isn't married."

Me, too. Tack had said he had no wife, but did I believe him? "I don't think so. But who knows?"

"Chin up, babygirl. It's his loss....Are you still doing that infomercial this week?"

My agent had gotten me a gig for my face to be used to promote a new skin care product a Dallas dermatologist wanted to market. A first for me. When he had approached me, wary of having products with which I was unfamiliar slathered all over my face, I said no. But in the end, I had succumbed to the money.

I closed my eyes and sucked up the last of my energy drink, making a loud slurping sound. I nodded. "Thursday and Friday."

Chad picked up the end of my pony tail. "Then before you do that, you need to go see Ashley, sweetie. Your ends are split. You need a trim and conditioning in the worst way."

"I know. I've got an appointment at two."

I went home, showered, put on my jeans and a sweater and threw a change of clothes, my sleep clothes and some toiletries in a weekend bag. Then I stashed my tip money in my purse and headed for the beauty salon owned by Ashley Harrison. She was more than my BFF. She was my go-to girl when it came to men and sex. Being seven years older than I, she was more like a big sister. I hadn't seen her in a couple of weeks.

Ashley's shop, Tangles, was located in a nondescript strip center, but on the inside, it looked like an elegant Grecian temple. It was small and intimate, with only three other stylists besides her. It had a spa in the back room. Hairstyles or nails or spa treatments from Tangles didn't come at bargain basement prices.

Ashley greeted me with a hug. I took a seat in her chair and she draped me with a black plastic cape, giving me a big grin in the mirror. She was all Italian—deep brown eyes, full red lips, flawless olive skin and a cloud of black hair she wore in a long curly-all-over do. Everyone told her she looked like Cher. She had been transplanted in Texas as an infant when her parents moved here from New Jersey. She was the best hairdresser I had ever had.

"So what are we doing for you today, Miss Miranda?"

"Nothing exotic. I'm doing that infomercial on Thursday and Friday, you know, so I think simple is best. Also, I'm pressed for time. I'm driving to Roundup when I leave here. My little sister has lost control of Mom again."

"Uh-oh. Sounds dangerous."

"Tell me about it." We walked together to her shampoo room.

On Mondays, she didn't have a shampoo girl. I took a seat at a shampoo bowl and she doused my head with warm water. I closed my eyes and drifted into my own little Nirvana as she proceeded to massage my tension away. I loved having my hair shampooed, especially by Ashley. Magic lived in her fingers.

"Can't wait to hear what you think of that skin doctor's product," she said. "I looked it up online. It's very expensive."

"I know. He's got it set up to sell on TV and the Internet with one of those subscription programs."

"Find out if he's going to market it in any shops. My ladies might be customers for something like that. For that matter, I've got guys inquiring about skin care. It's a big thing with men now."

I instantly thought of Gabe Mathison who was more concerned about his appearance than I was about mine.

"So what's going on with your mom?" Ashley asked.

"Same old thing. She was almost okay taking pills every day, but she woke up one day in the last few weeks and decided not to. I just found out about it."

"Lisa didn't let you know?"

"No, but I can't be mad at her. She doesn't get it where Mom's concerned. I don't think she ever tries to learn anything about bipolar disorder. It's like she's in denial."

"That is so sad, Miranda. I know you worry about her all of the time. What are you going to do?"

"I don't know yet. I have to go out there and take a look at the situation. I have to think about Lisa, too." Now Ashley was working her magic on my neck with strong fingers. "Oh, God, Ash, that feels so good."

She rinsed my hair, then applied something that smelled like coconut. "Hm. That smells like we should be eating it instead of putting it on our hair. Listen, seems like ages since we've talked. Is Angelo still moving in with you?"

"Next week. It'll be nice having a sexy guy who knows his ass from first base in my bed every night. At least he's Italian."

Angelo was a hot body and all male, all the time. He owned a successful restaurant construction business and traveled half the time. He had been trying to establish something more permanent with Ashley for several years.

Ashley continued. "But I haven't shared living quarters with another human being since I was married to Josh Harrison, who wasn't Italian, by the way. And that was a real long time ago."

Ashley was a thirty-five-year-old independent woman with a fiery temperament. When it came to men, her BS tolerance quotient was at basement-level. She had a skepticism streak a mile wide.

"Now, Ash. You know Angelo loves you. You have to give him a chance."

"Hah. It might not last a week. This is a very big deal for me. I'm going to have to kick Buffy Ann out of my bed, poor baby. Angie says he doesn't like a large rat sleeping with us. I hope hurting Buffy Ann's feelings turns out to be worth it."

Buffy Ann was a demanding Yorkshire terrier that might weigh five pounds soaking wet. Ashley unrepentantly spoiled her. I smiled in the mirror. "And he'll learn to love Buffy Ann, too."

"We'll see. How did the thing for Drake Lockhart go? I hear the real estate market is getting hot again. Lots of rich people coming from out of state and falling all over themselves to spend their money, am I right?"

From out of nowhere, tears flooded my eyes. My purse sat on my lap. I grabbed it and pawed inside for a Kleenex.

Ashley paused, her eyes wide with concern. "Miranda, what's wrong?"

I shook my head. "I'm okay. Ignore me."

I fell into a full-fledged wail, sopping tears from my eyes with a tattered Kleenex. "I screwed up so bad, Ashley. Saturday, I met this guy at Skyline. He's a friend of Drake's. He was just so damn good-looking and sexy. He came on to me hard. I thought we had a connection. Oh, Ash, I let myself be seduced. I spent the night with him at the Hilton. I did things with him I've never done with any man, not even Donald."

"Oh, Donald Sloan. *Phfft.*" She flopped her hand at me. "If you hadn't told me so, I wouldn't have believed he even had a dick."

Ashley had never been a big fan of Donald's. She sat me upright in the chair and wrapped my head with a thick towel. "I thought you hated men these days."

"I do."

"So why are you crying? It didn't go well or what?"

"It was wonderful. *He* was wonderful. He rocked my world all the way to my toes. I thought something clicked and I would hear from him again." On a deep sniff, I shook my head. "But he hasn't called me. I guess, to him, it was nothing more than a quick fuck while he was out of town."

"Aww. Are you sure? But hey, I'm not surprised, Miranda. That's the way a lot of guys are these days.

Wham, bam, thank you ma'am." She paused and frowned. "Well, a lot of them don't even add the thank you. That's why I say take no prisoners."

"I usually don't get drawn in like that. He caught me in a weak moment....Oh, Ashley, I really thought he'd call me."

"Bad form not to call. Just goes to show you he's a jerk. You did the safe sex routine, right?"

Inside, I winced. I hadn't yet let myself think about that part of Saturday night.

Relieving me of that disturbing thought, Ashley said, "Where does he live?"

"Midland."

I brought my tears under control and blew my nose. I didn't know where this weeping was coming from. I rarely cried. I prided myself on a cast-iron constitution. I wiped my eyes. "This is ridiculous. Hell, he probably has a wife and ten kids. He's too good-looking to be single."

"Wow," Ashley said, shaking her head. "How long has it been since you met a guy you liked?"

"A helluva long time. But I've learned my lesson. This won't happen to me again."

She led me back to her chair where I continued to unload my angst as she snipped my split ends away. She was the most patient listener I knew.

By the time she finished, my hair shone like a new penny. My mood still wasn't the best, but I felt better. I visited her bathroom, bought a Diet Coke from her vending machine, then left the salon and started west.

I reached Mom's house at nine, the same house in which I had spent the first eighteen years of my life. I didn't know exactly how old it was, but the floors and walls had old-fashioned linoleum and faded wallpaper, except for the kitchen and the one bathroom. Those two rooms had layers and layers of paint from years and years of re-dressing.

I was still in the driveway when Mom rushed out the front door and greeted me, her high heels sinking into the beige grass and weeds that passed for landscaping. No one ever cared for the yard. After it became so overgrown no one could stand to look at it, Lisa hired someone to mow. My grandmother would be sick if she saw it. She had always taken very good care of it.

Lisa trailed behind Mom, her posture showing a blasé resignation.

Mom looked frailer that the last time I had seen her several weeks back. And she looked uncharacteristically unkempt. She used to have deep red hair like mine, but now, due to her own attempts to maintain the color—and probably Lisa's, too—it was a multitude of shades ranging from gray to burgundy.

She fawned over me, patted my hair and hugged me again. She smelled of alcohol and Red Door, her favorite fragrance. "I'm so glad you're here, Miranda. I miss you so much. I wish you'd move back home."

Home. Though I had grown up in this house, it wasn't home to me without my grandmother in it.

Mom walked me toward the house with an arm around my waist. "Lisa doesn't know what to do about things. You always knew."

I had a lot of practice, Mom. "Lisa said you kicked Arnie out?" I said.

She gave a dismissive gesture. "Oh, he's nothing but a drunk. He's been getting on my nerves for a long time. I don't know why I ever married him."

She had said almost the same words about her previous husbands. We passed through the front doorway. The house had no designated entryway, so we walked directly into the living room.

"How was your drive?" Lisa asked. "You hungry?"

Startled by my surroundings, I turned in a circle, staring at the living room walls. The aged pastel green and blue floral wallpaper had been torn off in strips in some areas and patches in others. Two walls were sloppily half-covered with deep purple paint.

I didn't have to be told this was the result of Mom getting off her meds. An example of one of her manic episodes, although a benign one compared to some in the past.

All of my woes over my one-night-fling with Tack Tackett flew out of my head. Compared to my mother's issues that sooner or later became mine and Lisa's, a one-night-stand with a self-centered asshole didn't even hit the worthy-of-consideration mark.

The only words that came to me were, "What the hell happened here, Lisa?"

My sister came over and stood beside me. She and I were the same height, but that was where the similarities in our appearance ended. She was dark haired, dark eyed and square-built like her father.

She gestured at the purple wall. "Mom's redecorating."

She turned to our mother who stood with her eyes downcast, toying with the hem of her floaty top. Mom had always worn soft floaty clothing.

I withheld a huge sigh. Mom wasn't crazy. She knew right from wrong and she was usually contrite over the off-the-wall things she did. Without a doubt, she had known she shouldn't do this to the living room walls, but she had done it anyway. The illness was like a demon inside her. No one living outside her head had ever been able to control it. All my grandmother and I had been able to do was a poor job of managing it. When I had lived here, even though I had been a kid, much of the time, I had been able to cajole and talk her out of some crazy antic—except for men and marriages.

"She was celebrating Arnie leaving," Lisa said. "Covering up any sign that he had ever been here." Lisa gave Mom an elbow to the ribs. Out with the old, in with the new, right Ma?"

"When did she do this?"

"A week or so ago....While Arnie was in jail."

Mom lifted her chin. "You two please do not talk about me like I'm not here," she said indignantly.

I turned to her. "Why did you stop that medication, Mom?"

"Miranda, I refuse to let that silly old fart of a doctor ruin my looks. And I told him so. Why, he's not a doctor. He's just a—an old fart." An errant ringlet of red and gray fell across her eye. "I will not let him make me fat. You girls don't know what it's like."

What *what* was like? Being fat or dealing with her state of mind? I turned back to Lisa. "Why didn't you tell me about this sooner?"

"She seemed like she was gonna be okay. I didn't see any point in bothering you."

Mom looked down her nose at Lisa and drew a deep breath.

How many times had I been through situations like this? More talk failed me. "God. I need a drink of water." I stalked toward the kitchen, saying as I went, "Y'all got any clean glasses?"

I found a glass in the rubber dish drainer on the counter, ran it full from the faucet at the sink and carried it to the table. Made of chrome and gray Formica, the kitchen dining set had belonged to our grandmother. It had been in this same spot since I was a child. I eased down onto a chair at the end of the table.

Having followed me, Lisa took a seat adjacent to me.

"Where's Mom?" I asked her.

"She's still watching her TV show. It's one she likes. Nothing will keep her from watching it. How long are you staying, Miranda?"

"I'm going home tomorrow afternoon. I've got a couple of birthday parties booked and I'm filming an infomercial later this week."

"You're always so busy."

"I do stay busy. That's for sure."

"Now that you're here face-to-face, I need to talk to you about something. Remember Jessica Barlow from when I was in high school? She's moving to Abilene. She wants me to move with her and share expenses."

Crap! The day I'd been dreading was upon me. Lisa's wanting to bail didn't really come as a surprise. In the back of my mind, I had always known she wouldn't, or couldn't, hang in with Mom forever. I couldn't criticize. I hadn't been able to do it myself. I had tried to compensate for my absence by providing money.

"How are you going to do that? You don't have a job."

"I'll get one."

"Well..." I dragged out my reply, trying to come up with answers for all of us. "I guess you gotta do what you gotta do, Lisa."

"You're not mad?"

I shook my head. "How could I be mad? You've stayed here and taken care of her and put up with her husbands."

"Husbands aren't the only guys she drags in, you know."

Mom had never had a problem attracting men. "I know how she is, Lisa. The point is you're entitled to a life. And God knows, there isn't much of one for a twenty-two year old single woman in Roundup. When do you want to move?"

"I'd like to go in the next couple of weeks. I want to get settled before the holidays. I'm gonna try to get on somewhere waiting tables."

Lisa had no education beyond high school. At times I felt guilty about that. For all practical purposes, she'd had no guidance except from my grandmother and I'd had very few talks with her about her future. But that was a conversation for another day. Having no idea what her opportunities for work might be in Abilene, I simply nodded.

"What's the deal with Arnie?" I asked. "Do you think he's really gone for good?"

She nodded. "After Mom kicked him out, he hasn't even tried to come back. She was driving him crazy. Just like she does everybody."

"I suppose a divorce is next."

Lisa shrugged. "You can do it online. A friend of mine did."

"We'll see." Sighing, I stood. "I'm starving. What have you got to eat around here?" All I'd had all day was a protein bar, Chad's energy drink and a couple of Cokes.

"Not much," Lisa answered.

Inside the pantry, I found a can of Vienna Sausage. I carried it back to the table, opened it and dug the small sausages out with my fingers. I was so hungry for solid food they tasted like gourmet fare.

Lisa left the table and pulled a box of saltines out of the cabinet and brought it back. Pushing the box toward me, she watched me warily. "So what about Mom?

"What about her?"

"If I move, who's gonna take care of her?"

"She isn't helpless. If she stays on the medication and doesn't drink, she gets along okay."

"Who's gonna keep her from drinking if she wants to? If she gets back on those pills, who's gonna make her stay on them? She can't work or anything, Miranda. You know that. She really can't live by herself either. God, she's been so crazy lately, it wouldn't surprise me if she set the house on fire."

In spite of understanding why Lisa wanted to leave, I couldn't keep from blaming her for this latest episode. "Obviously not you," I said.

"What was I supposed to do, Miranda? Force them down her throat?"

Our mother appeared in the doorway. "I probably should go to bed, Miranda. If you really think I should take those pills, I will."

On some level that I or anyone else would never reach inside Mom's head, she knew the uproar she had created and she was sorry. With her being off the meds altogether for a couple of weeks, I was reluctant to advise her to take them now without advice from the doctor. "Let's wait another day, Mom. I'll catch up with that doctor tomorrow morning and see what he says."

∞

I awoke the next morning more tired than when I had gone to bed. I had spent the night planning and making some decisions.

My first task was to reach Mom's doctor, which I did easily. I had to wonder just how hard Lisa had tried. He wasn't a psychiatrist. He was the local family doctor who took care of everybody in Roundup. He instructed me to bring Mom into his office as soon as possible. Once we were there, he prescribed a new and different drug regimen to combat the depression he concluded she had fallen into.

At the only drugstore in town, I picked up Mom's new prescriptions and used some of the cash I had secreted in my purse to pay for them. I gave the rest of the money to Lisa as leaving-home-money.

Back at the house, I sat down with Mom and Lisa at the kitchen table and discussed the new pills. At the end of it, I turned to Mom and said, "Lisa wants to move to Abilene, Mom. I want you to come and stay with me in Fort Worth for a while." I avoided saying the word, "live."

"That would be nice, Miranda, but I couldn't possibly do that. Why, I can't leave this house empty."

"What if we sold it? Then you'd have some spending money."

I had been away from Roundup so long I didn't know if a real estate market existed here. I looked at Lisa. "Is there a real estate agent in this town?"

She shrugged. "One, I think."

"I'd have to think about that," Mom said, her eyes tearing. "This is all I have left of my mama. I don't know if I can give it up. It's bad enough I had to give *her* up." She began to cry.

My softer side empathized. My grandmother had been a giant of a woman, though she weighed only ninety pounds. She had survived as a widow for more than forty years, supported herself with no help in a tiny rural town with no economy. In my youth, she had been the only stable, dependable human being I knew.

"But you should be smart, Mom. One of these days Roundup is going to be a ghost town and you won't even be able to give this place away, much less sell it."

She turned her head and gazed out the window, still crying and wiping her eyes and nose. "I'm such a burden to everybody. Y'all would all would be better off if I wasn't here."

I reached for her thin hand that felt cold as ice and brought her attention back to me. "Not true, Mom," I said softly. "We'd miss you. I love you. And I'll take care of you. I always have."

A preview of what I was letting myself in for scrolled through my mind. But what choice did I have? Put her into an institution of some kind? Even if I were willing to do that, I couldn't afford it. If I found her a more qualified doctor, or doctors, in Fort Worth, she might get better faster. I had to believe that.

"Listen, let's cheer up around here. It's lunchtime. I want you to go get dressed up, Mom. Make yourself look pretty. I'm going to take you and Lisa out to lunch before I go back to Fort Worth. Okay?"

My mother had always loved to primp. Once, she had spent copiously on cosmetics and skin care products. She still did spend more than she could afford. God knew, I had heard about it from Lisa at different times. She must have passed that vanity gene on to me because I, too, spent freely at the cosmetic counter.

I took them to eat lunch at Roundup Cafe, the only place to dine out in Roundup besides the Dairy Queen. Afterward, we shopped for groceries and I bought a heaping basket of food. I dropped Mom and Lisa back at Grandma's house, my head already spinning with all that I had to do to prepare for Mom to move into my condo. Among other things, I had to find a babysitter to stay with her during the hours I wasn't at home.

Privately, I told Lisa, "You could call up that real estate agent and talk to him about selling this old house. And you could start packing Mom's things. I'll arrange for a moving truck or something."

Lisa was in a better mood and more compliant now that I had shown no anger at her wanting to go. It occurred to me that I should perhaps move her to Fort Worth and give her a job in my business. But one mountain at a time was all I could climb, so I put that thought on hold.

Then I was on the road back to Fort Worth, preoccupied with thoughts and memories of my mother. She had been so beautiful in her youth, I had once thought of her as a fairy princess. Now, the beauty was fading. She was a forty-five-year-old woman with no skills, no means of support and no money in the bank. And she was a victim of a terrible affliction. She had wreaked havoc in many people's lives through the years, including mine. Fortunately, she hadn't given birth to more kids, though it wasn't from a lack of trying. In my more cynical moments, I had diagnosed my mother as a good candidate for sterilization.

Mom was seventeen when I was born. For the first five years of my life, she had been a single mother. To this day, I had no idea who or where my father was. If Grandma knew, she had gone to her grave with the secret.

I was five and Mom was the age Lisa was now when she got married the first time and Husband #1 moved us to Las Vegas. Some days, Mom had taken me shopping in the most expensive department stores and I thought we were rich beyond measure. Later, I learned she had spent money like there was no tomorrow, lost thousands in the casinos and accumulated a $50,000 credit card debt her truck-driving husband had no hope of repaying.

When I was seven, Lisa was born. Soon after that, Husband #1 was gone and we never saw him again. I hadn't yet started school. Ostensibly, we had moved from Las Vegas to Roundup to live with my grandmother so I could become educated. But I believed the truth was that Mom recognized the monster within herself. She knew she couldn't be trusted to take care of me and Lisa and she had no way to support us. If not for my grandmother, I don't know what would have happened to my sister and me or Mom either.

After that, Mom had never been able to hold any kind of job for very long. Or stay married. Husband #2 had been a reasonably good man as far as I recalled, but, like the others, he must have run out of patience dealing with Mom on a daily basis.

As I drove through the monotonous landscape, childhood recollections flashed in and out of my mind, along with more current memories of Tack Tackett.

Just forget him, my wise inner voice told me. *He's shown you what he thinks of you. And stop checking your phone for calls from him. You'll never hear from him again. And you aren't going to have time to fool with him.*

That voice of good sense was right, of course. Besides being breathtakingly good-looking and even charming in a chauvinistic way, Tack was such a typical one-hundred-percent alpha male. Blunt and never revealing what he was thinking. If I spent enough time with him, no doubt he would get around to calling me "darling" or "honey." For some damned reason, I had always found that macho attitude irresistible. And it was in total conflict with my convictions as an independent woman.

I pulled into the driveway at my condo knowing I would be late getting to Smoky Joe's. I changed clothes and arrived at the cocktail lounge at 4:30 in body, if not in spirit. My boss, Joe, who was rarely seen in the lounge, was there. He and Winter, the cocktail waitress, both asked me if I was sick. I must have looked worse than I thought.

Cheery customers began to drift in. They distracted me from my woes. A nice man who had often asked me out sat at one end of the bar most of the evening entertaining me with jokes and clever conversation. He left me a hundred-dollar-tip. Why I had always declined his invitations to dinner I didn't know. When I counted my tips at the end of the evening, I'd had a good night.

On Wednesday, I dove into a long to-do list. I called the two college students who would be conducting two different birthday parties for eight-year-olds and made sure they were ready. I wouldn't be able to work out on Thursday or Friday, so I strapped my MP3 player onto my biceps, plugged in my earbuds and set out on a fast walk around the complex where I lived. During fast walking, I had done some of my most creative thinking.

When I returned, I poached an egg for breakfast and toasted a piece of low-carb bread I bought at the health food store. Afterward, to set my mind in a more positive direction, I went shoe shopping at the mall near my condo. Neiman Marcus was having a sale.

Shopping always elevated my spirits. The mall already showed vestiges of Christmas mixed in with Halloween that was only days away. I tried a pair of elegant red pumps that would probably go with anything I bought to wear through the holidays. I already had several parties booked for December. As I handed the clerk my credit card, I thought about Tack and Christmas. Where would he be spending Christmas—hosting his sister and her family in the penthouse condo in Skyline? With other family members?

I was due to show up at a TV studio in Dallas at eight o'clock on Thursday for the first of two days of non-stop facials. The experience turned out to be interesting and educational. At the end of it on Friday, I came away with the silkiest, softest complexion I had ever had and a thick portfolio of professionally made photographs for which I had been granted rights to use, not to mention a nice paycheck. And my agent assured me this gig and the TV exposure would open doors for me for similar little jobs. If that were true, I hoped those opportunities hurried my way. I was twenty-eight years old. How much longer would I be lucky enough to have flawless, wrinkle-free skin?

On the weekend, I plunged into cleaning out the second bedroom in my condo and turning it into a place where my new roommate would be comfortable. I prevailed on my neighbor's two teenage sons to move my desk into my own bedroom. I hauled all of the clothes I had put in the second bedroom closet into my own overcrowded bedroom closet. I cleaned out the dresser and the chest. The whole time I worked, I lectured myself about my voluminous wardrobe and the money I spent on clothing. No one needed as many cocktail dresses as I owned or as many designer shoes. The only consolation was I took a good part of my clothing expense as a tax deduction. My CPA told me I was pushing the envelope, but doing it made sense to me. I wouldn't buy the dresses and shoes if I didn't need them for this or that event.

I no longer knew how much space Mom required, but she had always had a lot of clothes, shoes and cosmetics. I redecorated the room a little—a new comforter with a bright, colorful pattern, a new flat-screen TV.

I had worked at expunging Harvey O. Tackett from my brain, though on dark nights when I couldn't sleep, memories of his arms, his mouth, his tongue came back to haunt me, sort of like the handsome prince in a fairy tale. BOB no longer appealed to me.

I had been in touch with Lisa more often than usual, determined that nothing would interfere with the plan to sell my grandmother's house and move Mom away from Roundup. Lisa assured me that everything was still under control and Mom was prepared for the move. I planned to drive to Roundup on Saturday morning, meet with the real estate agent, help Mom list the house and bring her home with me on the same day.

Late on Friday, after returning from the grocery store, I was unpacking groceries when my doorbell chimed. I opened the door and saw a UPS truck driving away. A small square cardboard box had been left on the porch. The return address said *Hellman's, Midland, Texas.*

I didn't know what Hellman's was and the only person I knew in Midland, Texas, was Tack Tackett. The coincidence gave me pause for a second. The only thoughts I'd had about him the past week were the ones that had sneaked past my busyness and my defenses. Achieving that much had taken all of my will power. His dark, intense eyes and his words, though I now knew them to be phony, still overpowered my good intentions at unexpected moments.

With a frown of puzzlement, I carried the box into my living room. This was crazy. No one sent me presents. I sank to the edge of the sofa and tore open the box. Inside, I found a small ball of bubble wrap and an envelope. I carefully opened the envelope to see a note handwritten on what was obviously expensive paper.

> *To: Miranda the Beautiful*
> *I wanted to forget you, but I can't. I hope you haven't forgotten me. Something happened between us. I want us to see more of each other. Fingers crossed that you want the same. Please don't think I'm an ass for not staying in touch.*
> *Sincerely,*
> *Tack*

My heartbeat began to thud in my ears. Tears rushed in and blurred my sight. I slashed them away and unfolded the bubble wrap to reveal a package wrapped in silver paper and tied with a silver bow. I carefully removed the bow and the paper and found a soft gray velvet box. Inside it was a shiny silver cuff bracelet at least an inch wide and heavy. If it was real silver, it had cost him a dollar or two.

I studied it, looked for a marking or a signature, finally saw the tiny engraving on the inside: .925 Sterling. I also saw a larger engraving: *October 18, 2014.*

The date of the Lockhart Concepts open house, the day I met Tack Tackett.

I gasped and grabbed the note. As I re-read it, tears spilled over my eyelids.

My mother rushed into my head. Irresponsible, unpredictable and constantly in need of attention. And forever in need of someone to look after her. All packed and ready to move in with me.

I hurriedly pawed through the bubble wrap and paper looking for a phone number or an address, but found neither. I couldn't even call him or write him to thank him.

Oh, my God. What happens now?

About the Author

Anna Jeffrey is an award-winning author of contemporary romance novels with a mainstream flavor as well as zany romantic comedy/mystery. She has written 10 romance novels under the pseudonym of Anna Jeffrey and one as Sadie Callahan. She and her sister have co-written 7 comedy/mystery novels as USA Today Bestselling Author, Dixie Cash.

Anna Jeffrey's books have won the Write Touch Readers' Award, the Aspen Gold, and the More Than Magic awards. Her books have been in the finals in the Colorado Romance Writers award, the Golden Quill and Southern Magic as well as the Write Touch Readers' Award, the Aspen Gold and the More than Magic awards

She is a member of Romance Writers of America and NINC. She enjoys many hobbies, i.e., reading, painting and drawing, crafting, needlework and beading among others. She and her husband live outside a small town in North Central Texas.